Isorropia

Brian S Monroe

Published by books.bass-x.net. Catalog number KLB-017.
Revised First Edition.

DISCLAIMER:

Although real locations are used and referred to, none of the events or people in this story are based on or are intended to resemble any person, living, dead, or imaginary. This story is not based on any event that has occurred or will occur. Any resemblance to any person or event is an unfortunate coincidence.
Due to safety and security concerns, the procedures and policies described in the government agency scenes are not true-to-life. This includes references to personnel procedures. The location described is generic and not intended to portray a specific office.
The reference to Farb and the theory of the universe in balance is paraphrased from Peter Farb's *"Man's Rise to Civilization"* (E.P. Dutton, New York, 1968).

books.bass-x.net
Shelton Washington

ISBN: 0983885907
ISBN-13: 9780983885900
LIBRARY OF CONGRESS CONTROL NUMBER: 2011915145

DEDICATION

To Outre-7

"Ne Plus Ultra"

CONTENTS

ACKNOWLEDGEMENTS

I would like to express my deepest gratitude and warmest thanks to M. Rounsley, J. Andrew, and S. Minor for their invaluable criticisms, encouragement, and suggestions that helped me achieve the final form of the story.

1

TERROR AND INTIMIDATION

Megan looked up sharply toward the door that had just slammed shut. The echoes were still dying when Lisa reached the station next to her and collapsed in her chair—her eyes blazing with anger and tears, her jaw clenched, her face flushed scarlet.

She instinctively turned back to the lobby. The noise had startled the waiting customers into silence. They exchanged furtive whispers, staring at Lisa's station with wide eyes. Megan turned back to Lisa. She was trembling with rage, arms hugged tightly to her sides, fists clenched, staring fixedly at her computer screen.

"Lisa?" asked Megan, as softly as possible.

Lisa started at the sound of her voice but did not turn her head. Concerned, Megan reached over and laid her hand gently on her arm, flinching as she touched her.

Like ice, flashed through Megan's mind.

"Lisa? Why don't you just take your break now? I can go afterward. I think you need to get away from the counter for a bit."

Lisa gave a slight nod and pushed her chair back. She stood, then broke into a run, heading into the hallway. Her footsteps faded as Megan sighed and turned back to the customer in front of her.

The customer had a shocked look on her face.

"Is she all right?" the customer whispered.

Megan, fighting the urge to sprint after Lisa, nodded her head and managed to smile.

"Yes—she's just a little upset. Having a bad day. Now," she continued, "could you please read the letters on line one for me, left to right?"

The customer smiled back and turned her attention to the eye-testing device. A shadow of concern instantly passed across Megan's cheerful expression and she glanced around behind her as she continued the eye test. She recovered herself as the customer removed their head from the machine and was smiling as before.

Megan completed the transaction and sent the customer down to the camera area. She automatically hit the **CALL NEXT** button and the artificial voice began reeling off its litany: '*Now serving customer number 206 at station number four.*' An individual detached himself from the rows of chairs, making his way toward her.

She beckoned him forward, still looking distractedly behind her. As the customer reached her station, a male figure in uniform emerged from the shadows of the hallway. Megan jerked her arm in an attempt to get his attention, relief already flooding her face.

"Zack!" she mouthed without using her voice.

He looked at her and came over quickly as she turned back to her customer.

"What can I do for you today?" she asked.

"I need a copy of my driving record," he replied.

"Did you need it for employment, insurance—?"

"Insurance," the customer cut in.

"I'll need your ID please."

As the customer handed her his ID, she reached out for it and quickly turned to Zack who was now standing slightly behind her. His eyes widened as soon as he saw the expression on her face.

"What is it?" he asked in a quiet voice, looking around behind him.

She motioned for him to bend down. He leaned toward her as she turned back to her customer.

"Get back to the break room!" Megan whispered urgently. "Lisa just came out of the office and about took the door off the hinges."

She quickly typed in the customer's information.

"I wondered what that noise was," remarked Zack.

"That will be ten dollars, please," said Megan, as she handed back the ID. The customer took it and handed her a twenty-dollar bill in return. She pressed a key. A receipt silently appeared; one of the counter printers came to life and ejected a sheet of paper into its tray.

"Here is ten dollars change and your receipt. I'll be right back with your record," she said with a smile. She rose and stepped away quickly from her station toward the printer, Zack following at her side.

"Don't know what happened in there. She was *really* upset. I thought she was going to break down at the counter—tears and everything!"

Zack was dumbstruck.

"Lisa was *that* upset?"

"Yeah," said Megan, retrieving the driving record from the printer tray and turning back toward her station.

"You'd better talk to her," she finished and then, her attention focused on her customer, she returned to her station and handed over the driving record.

Zack stayed where he was for about a minute as though he had something else to say. Then he turned on his heel and walked swiftly back into the hallway.

Megan was in the middle of another transaction when she heard the unmistakable sound of the office door swinging open. She shuddered involuntarily, glancing nervously over her shoulder. She turned away quickly and attended to her customer as though unaware of what was going on behind her.

Her senses on the alert, she felt rather than heard the sound of someone stealthily approaching her station with steady, unhurried steps. The hair on the back of her neck tingled as the steps came closer. Despite her precautions, she jumped when the dry voice spoke behind her.

"Why aren't you on break?"

Megan did not turn around and continued to help her customer. She could feel an expression of stern disapproval burning itself into the back of her neck but she kept herself in check, strenuously resisting the temptation to look over her shoulder. She did not look behind her until her customer walked away from her station.

A woman stood there—a woman with a very discontented expression that was rapidly getting worse. A tall woman dressed severely in a monochrome suit that matched her ivory skin and jet-black hair perfectly. A woman with a taut figure that radiated a sense of power and menace. A woman whose black eyes glittered threateningly.

Megan shrank back into her chair.

"I asked you a *question*," the hard voice repeated.

Megan swallowed but met her eyes squarely.

"I switched with Lisa."

The woman's glare grew stronger. Advancing half a step closer, she said, "I don't recall being asked or approving that request."

Her voice was low and soft but it cut through the air like a razor blade. Megan resisted the temptation to cower and cover her ears.

"The Shop Steward wanted to talk with her."

The woman did not relax her gaze.

"Right *then?*" she asked.

Megan nodded.

"*Right* then."

A look of baffled rage flashed over the woman's face, her nostrils flaring. She raised her lips and sucked in her breath with a sharp hiss through exposed, clenched teeth. She turned away and strode deliberately back into her office, shutting the door behind her. Megan let out her breath in a sigh of relief.

"You ready for a break?"

Megan jumped. It was Zack.

"Yeah. Listen," she continued in a lower voice as she pulled her money out of the till, glancing furtively toward the office door. "I told her you had to talk with Lisa right away to cover why I didn't take my break on time."

His eyes flashed but he remained calm as he put his money in the till.

"Out for blood again, is she?" he remarked.

Megan nodded.

Zack's disgusted expression perfectly matched the tone of his voice.

"I am getting so *sick* of this. She's done enough damage already and now she wants to—"

"Sh!" whispered Megan urgently. "I'd better get out of here while I can. Is Lisa okay?"

Zack shrugged his shoulders.

"I hope so."

He faced the lobby, logged into the computer and called the next customer.

Megan walked rapidly down the hallway into the break room. There were two people sitting at the table—a man and a woman. They both looked up with alarm, then relief on their faces as she entered. Megan swiftly glanced around the room.

There was no sign of Lisa.

"Kip, Rolla, have you seen Lisa?" she asked, without any attempt to keep the concern out of her voice.

"She was sitting here crying and just ran out of here when we came in," said Rolla. Kip nodded.

"Where? Which way?" Megan's throat tightened.

"Toward the back," responded Kip, pointing further down the hallway.

Megan spun around and half-ran down the hallway to the outside door. She reached it and pushed it open, rapidly scanning to her left and right.

Still no sign of Lisa.

She slapped her hands against her sides with a gasp of frustration and turned around. Retracing her steps, she stopped at another door and peered through the glass into a room lined with tables and chairs.

The conference room was deserted.

Megan struggled to keep herself from panicking. Her palms sweating, her breathing shallow and her heartbeat pounding, she race-walked back toward the counter area and stopped dead in her tracks—frozen with terror.

She just missed colliding with the woman by seconds.

"Did I say *you* could take your break?" said the cruel voice. The woman's eyes were wide open, glaring with anger. Megan fought uselessly to maintain her poise. She stared at the face in front of her, soundlessly moving her blanched lips. Seeing this, the woman twisted her mouth in a sadistic smile.

"*Well?*" she demanded, louder.

Megan took a deep breath.

"*I* told her to take it!"

Both women whirled toward the source of the voice and found themselves face to face with Zack. He had dropped his subdued manner; his voice was hard, his eyes arctic. Megan looked at him with hope in her eyes, the woman with defiance in hers.

"Do you have a problem with that?" he asked, moving closer.

"No—whatever," the woman muttered, lowering her eyes as she pushed past him. Megan heard the office door close shortly afterward.

Zack's grim expression softened and he gripped Megan's shoulder briefly.

"You okay?" he asked.

Megan smiled faintly.

"*I'm* fine. What happened to Lisa?"

"What do you mean, '*what happened to her*'?" Zack responded, concern coming into his voice.

"I can't find her anywhere back there. Kip and Rolla said that she '*just ran out*' heading toward the back door when they came in."

Zack thought this over for a moment. His eyes widened suddenly.

"Get back to your station," he snapped sharply, "I'll go look for her."

He turned and ran rapidly down the hallway toward the outside door. Megan stared after him in dismay, then turned and walked back to her station. She took several deep breaths before she logged back in and called the next customer.

Three transactions later, she became aware of an unusual noise behind her growing louder. She turned around just in time to see Zack fly out of the hallway. The expression on his face chilled her to the core. He raced over to the office door and violently flung it open.

The outraged roar from within was instantly cut off as he entered, screaming, "You heartless, worthless—" and slammed the door shut behind him. There was the faint sound of an angry shouting match rapidly escalating—then absolute silence.

The door was suddenly jerked open disclosing Zack, his face crimson with fury and the woman right behind him. Megan stared at her: the usual arrogance in her expression was warped with—*was it concern? Annoyance? A mixture of both?* Megan could not decide. They both vanished into the hallway at a run.

Megan stared blankly after them until a sharp, "Hel*lo?*" from her station recalled her with a start. She quickly turned back to her customer who was regarding her sourly. She blushed.

"I'm sorry about that, sir," apologized Megan. "What can I do for you today?"

The customer curled his lip disdainfully and handed his license to her without a word. She took it and began typing.

A few minutes later, she heard the sound of sirens in the distance drawing rapidly nearer. It wasn't until she saw the flashing red and blue lights through the lobby windows that she realized they were responding to the parking lot. A cold flash of fear ripped through her body as she irrationally connected their arrival with Lisa's disappearance. She twisted in her chair and looked anxiously behind her, even as she reminded herself that there was no logical reason to associate the two events.

She forced herself to turn back around and continued to call up customers. But her wandering eyes drew unwillingly back to the semaphore of flashing lights through the glass in front of her again and again.

Eventually she glanced at the clock: twelve-thirty. Her stomach growling, she frowned and looked around her. Rolla was working two stations down; Kip was at the opposite end. Megan muttered under her breath and quickly typed an e-mail message:

Any idea when we're going to get lunch?

She sent it off to Rolla and continued assisting customers. The reply came a few minutes later:

Don't know. Drak and Shawn haven't come in yet.

Megan's frown increased. Ignoring her growing hunger pangs, she tried to concentrate on her customers. She was so absorbed that she missed the departure of the first responders. She happened to look up toward the window at one point and noticed the flashing lights were gone.

There still was no sign of relief for lunch.

It was nearly ten minutes to one when Megan heard a familiar voice calling to her from the lobby, "Hey there Megan! How are you today?"

Megan smiled, despite her exhaustion, at the woman walking toward her station.

"Hi Lilly," she replied.

Lilly, trim, beautiful with luxurious thick hair and vivid blue eyes, made her way to the counter as lithe as a dancer. It wasn't until she was closer that Megan caught the tension in her eyes.

"How are things going?" asked Lilly.

Megan lowered her voice discreetly.

"We haven't had our lunches yet—have no idea where the others are. It's been another ugly morning."

Lilly nodded distractedly as though she wasn't listening. Megan was shocked. *Something's wrong*, she thought to herself.

"Where is your boss?" asked Lilly, her eyes darting around the counter area.

Megan paled but answered firmly, "I don't know. She ran out back with Zack—about two hours ago. Haven't seen either of them since."

Lilly gave a brief smile, gently squeezed Megan's hand and walked purposefully toward the swinging gate. She waved to Rolla and Kip as she let herself through and made her way down the hallway.

A few minutes later, three figures emerged and approached the counter: Zack and two other men. Zack came up to her station; the other two approached Kip and Rolla respectively.

"Sorry about that," said Zack apologetically. Megan opened the till and pulled out her cash as Zack slipped his in. Her smile died at the sight of Zack's expression, twisting his face with anger and grief.

"What—?" she began and found she had to clear her throat before continuing.

"What's wrong?" she asked in a half-whisper.

Zack shook his head and pressed the **CALL NEXT** button.

"Is she okay?"

Zack turned and looked at her.

"I don't want to talk about it. *You* need to get your lunch," and, giving her a faint smile of reassurance, attended to the customer who had just reached his station.

Megan took a deep breath and half-stumbled, half-walked back the break room. She had to catch herself twice from dropping her lunch on the floor. It was a relief to finally sit down and let her primal instincts take over as she wolfed down her food. She only paused once to pour herself a hot cup of coffee. Rolla and Kip entered shortly afterward and busied themselves with their lunches.

"Everything okay?" came Lilly's voice from the doorway. They all looked up and nodded. Lilly smiled briefly with the same strained expression Megan noticed earlier. She quickly withdrew. All three of them looked at each other, amazed—they all read the same meaning in Lilly's eyes.

It was not comforting.

"Something's wrong," Rolla muttered, echoing Megan's thoughts earlier.

Kip nudged her and she looked up with a start. Megan instinctively turned around and froze. The woman was standing in the doorway, regarding them calmly. However, her gaze did not have its usual intimidating effect: something in her eyes had changed as though she was unwillingly restraining herself.

"Everything okay?" she asked, echoing Lilly's words with bitter parody.

They nodded silently.

She left without another word.

They exchanged bewildered looks, shrugged and continued eating.

At one-thirty, Megan rose up with a sigh and walked over to her locker. She opened it and pulled out her coat, her hat and her clipboard. She stepped out into the hallway and walked into the supply room where she found a stack of forms and papers. She picked up one of the papers and clipped it to the board. She was reaching for a pad of forms when Lilly's voice startled her.

"Megan? Can you come out here and work the counter?"

Lilly was standing in the doorway.

"I have a line of drives," replied Megan.

Lilly frowned briefly.

That's not like her either, thought Megan.

"How many lines are there this afternoon?" she asked.

"Two. Kip and I were scheduled."

Lilly's uncertain demeanor suddenly hardened.

She was undecided about something, Megan realized, *but not anymore.*

"Go back and tell Rolla I want *her* to take your drives. I need you to take over for Zack."

Megan nodded as Lilly vanished from the doorway.

Megan gave a sigh of displeasure and picked up the clipboard. She made her way back to the break room just in time to catch Rolla and Kip standing up from their chairs.

"Rolla?" she asked. Without waiting for an answer, she handed her the clipboard and forms. Rolla took them with an expression of surprise gradually passing to dismay as Megan continued.

"Lilly says you have to take my drives. I have to work the counter for Zack."

Without waiting for a response, she turned back and headed for the counter. She was almost to the end of the hallway when she caught Rolla's disgusted, "Great. *Just* what I wanted to do today," from the break room. Megan shrugged her shoulders and kept going. *She's as happy about it as I am.*

Zack was waiting for her. They switched out. She settled down and logged in. Zack quickly secured his cash and headed for the office. Lilly and the woman were waiting inside. The door shut quietly behind him.

The door did not open again until about an hour later. Zack emerged from the interior with a dark expression. He stood for a couple of minutes taking deep breaths—then retrieved his cash, Megan following him with anxious eyes.

He walked up to her station.

"Break time," he announced in a strained voice Megan failed to notice.

"But you're supposed to go first—" Megan protested but Zack roughly pulled her chair back from the station and snapped angrily, "Just *take* it, okay?"

Megan stared at him, her mouth open in shocked surprise as Zack forced her out of the chair, keyed open the till and ripped her money out while logging her out of the computer. He slid into her chair, slapped her money into her hand, and abruptly turned back to the computer, ignoring the hurt in her eyes, his fingers viciously pounding the keys as he logged in. He stuffed his money in the till, slammed it shut harder than he needed to and called the next number.

Megan recovered herself, her face burning and hurriedly left the counter area. She made her way to the break room and collapsed in a chair, curling up her head in her arms on the table. She lay like that for a while until she felt a soft hand on her head and heard Rolla's voice.

"You okay, hon?"

Megan slowly raised her head and met Rolla's gaze, her tear-filmed red-rimmed eyes blazing. Seeing her concern, Megan pushed herself up to a sitting position, leaning back in the chair.

"Yeah—just kind of upset," she stated with a weak smile, wiping her eyes and shaking her hair.

Rolla raised her eyebrows and sat on the opposite side of the table. Kip walked in and went over to the sink, drawing a glass of water.

"What's going on up front?" asked Rolla, still gazing at Megan curiously.

Megan silently shook her head.

"Is Lilly still here?" she persisted.

"Yeah. They're still talking in *her* office."

Megan stood up, stretched and walked out of the break room, ignoring Rolla's cry of, "Hey! Where are you going?" She walked back to her station with smoldering eyes. Zack had no idea she was standing behind him until she cleared her throat. He turned around in his seat and then looked at the clock, perplexed.

"That wasn't fifteen minutes," he began but stopped when he saw the look on her face.

"It's enough for *me*," said Megan acidly, "*Get out of there.*"

Zack arched his eyebrow, giving her a sharp glance. She returned his look coldly. Shaking his head in disbelief, he got up, pulled out his money and walked out without looking back.

Megan ignored him as she settled back in her chair and called the next number. Her resentment slowly faded away as she absorbed herself in her customers, the fire dying in her eyes.

Zack finished his break, returned and activated the station next to her, sliding into his chair and deliberately ignoring her. His troubled face betrayed his feelings; Megan caught herself looking over at him, worriedly. She fought the impulse for as long as she could before she finally leaned over and whispered to him:

"Are you okay?"

He gave a short laugh.

"What do *you* think?" he replied bitterly. She blinked but did not back down.

She waited a few more minutes before leaning over again and asking, "Is Lisa going to be all right?"

She shrank from the intensity of Zack's expression as he slowly turned toward her. It wasn't just anger she saw—there was something deeper added to the mix. It frightened her.

"I don't know," he finally said, enigmatically.

Megan's heart sank.

"What's going on in the office?" she asked, attempting to change the subject.

Zack shook his head.

"Don't want to talk *here*," he said, shortly.

Megan hesitated.

"After? The usual?"

Zack curled his lip but kept his voice civil.

"Yeah."

She said nothing more to him the rest of the afternoon.

Shortly afterward, she heard the office door open and Lilly's voice—her usual cheerful tone still sounding a bit forced.

"Zack? Can you come back in here?"

It was not a question: it was a *demand*. Zack locked his computer with a sigh and made his way back to the office, ignoring Megan's concerned look. The door shut once again.

The rest of the afternoon dragged on. At one point, she heard the sound of raised voices but even as she leaned back in her chair to hear better the sounds faded. She looked back toward the office anxiously but nothing was visible through the shaded window. She sighed and turned to the clock: four-twenty.

Still another forty minutes to go.

The office door still hadn't opened when Megan rose up from her chair, printed her closing reports and pulled her money out. She walked over to the printer, grabbed some papers waiting in the tray and made her way to the checkout room. She caught Rolla's eye and nodded her head.

"Starting checkout?" asked Rolla.

"Duh," responded Megan.

Megan counted her cash and checks, verified the amounts against the reports, smiled as she compared the expected balance to the actual balance and signed the forms.

She stepped to the doorway and called, "Rolla?"

Rolla nodded her head, finished up with her customer, then started printing her reports and brought back her cash. Megan counted it up and verified the totals.

"You want me to get Zack's money?" asked Rolla.

Megan hesitated.

"They still at it?"

Rolla nodded.

"I guess," she sighed reluctantly.

Rolla left and returned shortly afterward with Zack's reports and money. She counted and verified his deposit; Megan initialed.

"Might as well close out his machine," said Megan. Rolla nodded and went back to the counter.

There were still several customers waiting when the front door was locked forcing Drak and Shawn to remain at the counter while Rolla took pictures. Kip came in from doing drive tests and turned in his cash to Megan. Then Drak printed his reports and brought in his cash. The last customer finally departed and Shawn came in with his money.

"Go ahead and close out," said Megan to the others. They went out to their stations and closed out their machines for the day, shutting the computers down after receiving the confirmation code. Shawn—his money counted by this time—went out to his station and asked, "Has everyone closed out?"

"Yes," came the unanimous reply.

Shawn's fingers clacked the keyboard and a series of reports came out of the printer, Kip putting them in order as they emerged. He carried them back to Megan who was just completing the final deposit. She glanced at the total, checked her tape and gave the thumbs up sign.

Kip leaned out of the checkout room doorway and said "Good to go." Shawn cleared his station and closed out his machine. Lights were switched off, equipment powered down; there was a flurry of coats being donned, purses being slung and hats being set.

Megan finished the deposit and sealed the bag. She initialed the label, then Rolla countersigned it. The deposit secured and the checkout room locked, Megan called goodbye to Rolla who was already heading for the door. Rolla waved back at her without turning around.

Megan looked over the now deserted counter and sighed with frustration. The office door was still closed, the discussion unfinished. After waiting a few minutes, she pulled on her coat, zipped it shut and headed for the outside door. She resisted the sadistic impulse to arm the perimeter alarm system and walked out to the parking lot.

It was already dark and a cold wind blew fitfully as she walked across the parking lot, her hands deep in her pockets. Megan shivered a little and pulled the coat closer to her. Despite the chill, she was glad to be free of the stifling atmosphere of the office. The fresh air revived her spirit and much of the darkness that had gathered in her thoughts during the day faded away without leaving a trace.

She turned quickly as she heard the outside door opening. Zack and Lilly came out together. Even from this distance, Megan could see their expressions. She did not like what she saw and felt something of her forgotten anxiety return. She turned away to try to distract her thoughts and found herself looking at something strange on the pavement of the alleyway that ran behind the office.

Curious, she walked a little closer to it. She recognized it a few seconds later and brought herself to a quick stop.

It was the chalk outline of a body.

It hadn't been there earlier in the day—which meant that the incident had taken place sometime after the morning break. She found herself wondering what could have happened—as some of the possibilities occurred to her she shivered and turned away, not wanting to speculate any further.

Zack was standing in front of the door by himself, anxiously looking around the parking lot. Megan smiled to herself and walked toward him, waving her arm. He saw her and quickly came over.

"Wondered where you'd got to," he greeted her.

"I was just over there," she said, pointing behind her.

Zack frowned at that but quickly put the moment behind him and cleared his face.

"Where do you want to talk?" he asked.

"Well, your place maybe?"

Zack's face hardened.

"We've already gone there. Let's not go back there again," he said flatly, without looking at her.

Megan shook her head, irritated.

"*Jeezus* Zack, give me a break! *How* long has it been? *Ten* years? *Twelve?* Can't you let it go by now?"

He just looked at her silently.

"Fine. Whatever," she snorted, turning away from him and crossing her arms. She remained in that position silently for a few minutes, not moving.

"You feel like walking in the park for a while?" he asked after a few minutes.

She shrugged her shoulders.

"Sure. It's not *too* cold and windy," she spat, as she turned around, glaring at him.

He was too preoccupied to notice and began to walk toward the front of the building. She fell into step with him, linking arms as they turned the corner. They crossed the street to the park and strolled along the pathways, at peace for the moment.

"I'm sorry about that business earlier," he said suddenly, catching her by surprise.

"What business?" she asked, not remembering.

He flushed.

"You know—when I made you take your break."

"Oh!"

She had forgotten it by then.

"I'm really sorry about that," he repeated but she squeezed his arm in hers.

"Don't worry about it. I got the impression you were stressed out."

"*Oh* yeah," he agreed.

They walked in silence for a while.

"How is Lisa?" she asked suddenly. She felt his arm stiffen.

"I have no idea," he replied in an empty voice.

"Where is she?"

Another pause.

"Hopefully in Intensive Care."

Megan felt as though she had been pushed into a pool of ice water.

"What—what happened?" she quavered.

Zack hesitated.

"I don't know for sure," he said finally.

"All I know—or rather all I saw—" he made a growling noise in his throat.

"The facts are that she ran out of the back door straight into the path of one of those idiots taking a shortcut through the back alleyway. He must have been doing fifty when he hit her."

Megan came to a halt, the color drained from her face.

"Oh—gawd," she moaned.

Zack shook his head, miserably.

"The guy never had a chance to stop. She was knocked about—"

"I saw where they found her," cut in Megan quickly.

"She was alive when they got her in the ambulance but she was banged up pretty bad."

They started walking again.

"Why did she *do* that?" breathed Megan.

Zack's face was grim.

"The police are treating it as an unfortunate accident."

"And you?"

He stopped and looked at her.

"I think she did it on purpose."

Megan stared at him wildly.

"Why—?" she began in a barely audible voice.

"I can't prove it. I have nothing to back me up. But after what she told me this morning, it makes sense. She was pushed over the edge and couldn't take it anymore."

"So we've lost another one," said Megan softly.

Zack nodded.

"Yeah, that—" and he stopped himself, then began again, "That *witch* has claimed another victim," he spat out, bitterly.

"As soon as I heard her story this morning I called Lilly right away. I told her that if she didn't do something—but she got here too late. I had no idea Lisa was that far gone or I would never have left her alone in the break room. Oh, *blast* it!" he exclaimed angrily, smacking his palm with his fist.

"So now we have to start all over," said Megan as though to herself. "Another two months of advertising the position, choosing candidates, conducting interviews—and in the meantime we're down one person. No one is going to transfer here—not with the reputation *she* has."

"Yeah," Zack agreed, shaking his head in disgust, muttering under his breath.

"What went on in the office?" asked Megan after a while.

"*That* was interesting," replied Zack sarcastically. "I told both of them flat out that the situation here is out of control and it can't continue any longer. I said if they didn't do something, I'd request an investigation *and* file a grievance. I'm afraid I didn't put it very nicely but I just don't give a damn anymore."

"*Wow.* What did they say?"

Zack smirked.

"*She* was already looking daggers at me because I snitched on her to Lilly—*again*. She looked even more deadly after I put her on notice that any hint of retaliation was going to land her in court. I even got Lilly pissed off because I was talking about getting the civil-rights folks involved. We had some ugly exchanges in there."

"Good grief!" exclaimed Megan.

"Anyway, I emphasized that Lisa was going to be the last person browbeaten out of here. There will be *no* 'next time.' I made it clear that if they didn't like what I had to say they would have *another* position to fill."

Megan turned pale.

"Zack, you can't afford to quit—"

"You aren't telling me anything I don't know already. But I'm not going to stand by and watch her destroy people anymore. It's got to stop—*I'm* going to see that it does."

Megan was silent.

"Anyway, after they talked by themselves I got called back in and was told that my demands would be met. And Lilly made it clear I was to let her know if any more problems developed. But—"

"What?" prompted Megan after a few moments.

"I don't trust her. She looked at me like she wanted me cut alive into little pieces and dipped in salt water," he shuddered.

Megan shivered with him.

"How are *you* able to stand up to her?" asked Megan.

"I don't let her get the upper hand. You can't back down with a person like her. You give one inch of ground and she'll bring you down like lightning. You stand up to her she'll respect that. She still won't *like* you but she'll at least back off."

"Easy for you to say," remarked Megan bitterly. "You're a guy—you've got an edge that we don't. She's always going to go easier on you than us."

Zack stared at her, a look of derision twisting his face.

"Being a guy cuts no special advantage with her. Ask Lisa about that."

"What do you mean by *that?*"

"Well the whole reason why Lisa—" then he caught himself as though he had said too much and went silent.

"It doesn't matter," he said, finally. "You don't want to know."

Megan glared at him and tossed her head but he ignored her and kept walking.

"It isn't going to make any difference anyway," muttered Megan. "Nothing ever happens to *her.* She'll get away with this like she does everything else."

"You don't know that for a fact," remarked Zack.

"Oh *please*—don't start *that* up again," she exploded, pulling her arm away. "You always talk about how everyone eventually gets what they deserve but *I've* never seen it. People aren't dragged away by the statue in the last act in real life. They die fat, dumb and happy!"

"That's not true," remarked Zack, calmly.

"What do you mean *'it's not true'*? It damn well is—!" She was nearly screaming now.

"I mean, you don't *know* if they're happy. You can tell if someone is fat—that's easy. It's something you see right in front of you. But happy? The only way you can tell if a person is happy is if you can read their mind. And no one can do that."

Megan fought back an impulse to viciously wipe her hand across his face.

20

"They may *look* like they're happy," he continued in the same pedantic tone as before. "But that doesn't mean that they *are.*"

Megan walked on in wounded silence. Zack did not take any notice of her and kept looking straight in front of him.

"She *isn't* going to get away with it again," he said, finally.

The tone of his voice was so convincing she stopped, staring at him incredulously. Startled, he stopped too and returned her stare.

"How can you say that?" she asked, almost in a whisper.

"Because the universe will not allow it."

Megan rolled her eyes and turned to go with a sigh.

"No—seriously," he continued, "The universe," and he blushed but continued despite her rising eyebrows and increasing derision in her face, "the universe demands balance. You can only push it out of balance so far before it will right itself. It's like a coiled spring. Push too far and the recoil might throw you across the room—never mind!" he finished curtly as he saw her break into a smile. He turned abruptly and rapidly walked away.

She was only thrown for a moment.

"Hey!" she shouted and ran after him, catching up and grabbing his arm. He stopped and turned to face her, roughly pulling his arm free. Her eyes flared at this but she remained where she stood, their eyes locked together.

"Balance?" she repeated to him, as though prompting.

He sighed heavily and tried to turn away again.

"What do *you* care? Why should I bother to try to explain it to you? You never did—" and he caught himself again, locking his jaws together with a snap. He breathed deeply and closed his eyes for a moment.

Megan did the same.

"Have you ever read Farb?" he finally asked.

She frowned.

"No—never heard of him."

"Not surprising. Neither has anyone else," he remarked, bitterly.

"Well what about him?" she asked, defensively.

Zack hesitated as though trying to pick the right words to make his point.

"Well—he wrote a book about the First Peoples. I had to read it in college for a class. It was pretty fascinating. But his chapter on this one group really—it really reached me for some reason."

She was silent.

"You know I was born on a Reservation," he added. She raised her eyebrows at this.

"I didn't know that," she said, slowly.

He nodded.

"My parents still have my crib in storage somewhere. We have a blanket and—" and again he stopped himself. "Sorry, I'm running off the track," and he blushed.

Megan softened a bit.

"It's okay," she said shortly. "Go on."

"Well—this group he was describing believes that the entire universe is like a web—everything is connected together. And if anything causes stress on a part of that web, it causes counter-stress on the other parts of it. Like a spider web, you know?"

She did not respond.

"All of it is in a state of balance. Perfect balance. And it always tries to maintain itself in that state. It resists any attempts to throw it off—" and his voice faded as he caught the look in her eyes. He turned his head away.

"I can't explain it to you. I can't even explain it to myself. I just know that she can't get away with what she's doing forever. Something will happen—we might not get to see it or hear about it—but it will. I *know* it will."

She stared at him for a moment and then gave a short, sneering laugh. His eyes glared and he turned away, thrusting his hands in his pockets.

"Zack," she asked, half-mocking and half-serious, "Do you *really* believe that?"

He nodded his head but did not turn around.

Megan spoke slowly, staring straight ahead of her.

"*My* world has been out of balance for a long time," and she suddenly looked right at him, her eyes glinting with anger.

"*Too* damn long, Zack. I think it will be easier for me to believe you if I actually see it happen to *me* first."

Zack straightened himself up and quickly walked away from her without turning around.

She laughed harshly; he quickened his pace. Annoyance flooded her face and she angrily placed her hands on her hips.

"Sorry to waste your time," she shouted sarcastically. She turned around and swiftly walked back to the office parking lot. She did not look behind her to see if he was following. She found her car, got in and drove off, fury clouding her eyes.

2

POINT/COUNTERPOINT

It was Monday when the phone rang. *Early* Monday. The electronic summons knifed its way into Megan's subconscious like a white, hot, lightning bolt of pain. At first she tried to ignore it. She fought the urge to wake up as long as she could and then came to herself, tangled in the blankets, struggling and gasping for breath. She angrily thrust them aside, shivering as their warmth vanished.

The phone continued to ring.

She fumbled and managed to grab it from the charger without dropping it. She glared furiously at the Caller ID display for nearly two more rings before she recognized the number. She flashed into full alertness and punched the **TALK** button.

"Yes?" she asked, breathlessly.

"Got some news for you," Zack said, tonelessly.

Her unreasoning excitement quickly cooled down although her heart still pounded loudly in her ears. She gritted her teeth and clenched her toes, trying to stifle her disappointment.

"Oh?" she asked, sounding casual.

"I got a phone call," he continued, "from Donna."

Megan instinctively hunched her shoulders and looked around furtively as though afraid she'd be overheard. She was immediately angry with herself for overreacting and alarmed at how deep her fear was embedded.

Whipping her hand through her hair, she asked, "What did—what did she say?"

He sighed audibly over the phone.

"Lisa resigned."

Megan went cold.

"Zack—" she faltered but he cut in immediately.

"I don't know, Megan. They won't let anyone see her now. I don't know what's going on. Her attorney handed in the paperwork to HR on Friday. I only found out about it just now."

"Oh gawd—" said Megan in a flat, shrunken voice.

"Was there anything else you wanted to tell me?" she asked when the silence began to get awkward.

"Yeah—good news. It looks like we won't have to go through the interview thing after all."

"Why?" she asked, not understanding.

"Someone transferred in," said Zack.

From the tone of his voice, it sounded like he didn't believe it anymore than she did.

"Who on earth transferred in?" she asked, incredulous.

"Guy named Mark Brock."

"How did he know the position was available that quickly?"

Zack sounded a little bitter.

"HR supposedly posted the position Wednesday. She didn't choose to explain why *we* weren't notified and I didn't feel like arguing with her at four-thirty a.m. I also got the impression that she knew about Lisa's resignation in advance, too. Or maybe it was HR that knew about it, I don't remember. All I know for sure is that they kept us in the dark—as usual."

She nodded as though he were there to see it.

"Zack, who *is* this guy? Where is he from?"

"Dunno. One of the offices up north I think. I'm not sure which one."

There was silence.

"Megan, are you there?"

"Yeah," she responded. "I'm just trying to think—" and she fell quiet again.

"Zack," she said after a moment. "Zack, there is no *way* he couldn't have heard about her. The whole *region* knows about her. I mean if he were coming from the eastern side I could understand—but why would he want to come down here after hearing—"

"I have no idea," Zack replied, wearily. "He's already starting off on the wrong foot."

"How's that?"

"She left a message for him to call and confirm he was taking the position. He called her at home about an hour ago."

Megan thought for a moment and then burst out laughing hysterically. Zack joined in briefly.

"Oh my gawd!" she said when she could breathe.

"Yeah, rousted her up at four."

She could tell from the tone of his voice he was grinning.

"I suppose she got her revenge by calling you right afterward," said Megan.

"Yeah. To the second."

Megan leaned back on the pillow, a smile on her face.

"So what is this guy like? Have you heard of him before? *I* haven't."

"Have no idea," Zack replied. "We'll be seeing him tomorrow anyway and find out for ourselves. Have a good one," and before she could say anything he terminated the call leaving her staring at the phone with her mouth hanging open.

That son of a bitch! she thought to herself—but she couldn't stop smiling as she gently replaced the phone in its charger.

The nightstand clock said five forty-five.

She turned over and fell back into a dreamless sleep.

She did not hear from Zack for the rest of the day. Despite her resentment over his brusque termination of the phone call, she made an effort to get to work ahead of the others and pulled into the parking lot a good hour and a half before reporting time. However, Zack was already there ahead of her—or at least his car was. And there was one other car as well—a car she had never seen before.

She gave it an appraising glance as she walked toward the entrance. *Impressive*, she thought to herself. It wasn't new, probably two or three years old, but the paint was glowing, the chrome gleaming and the tires a glossy, sparkling jet-black.

The license plate caught her attention before she got to the door. It was a personalized plate that read: **ISORPIA**.

Usually it wasn't hard to pick out the meaning behind the acronyms on personalized plates but this one had her puzzled. She found herself muttering the phrase repeatedly under her breath as she keyed open the back door and walked into the break room.

Zack was at the table keeping company with a steaming cup of black tea. He looked up briefly as she entered and immediately looked away. Megan would likely have said something to him had her eyes not been arrested by his table companion who rose from his chair as she came into the room.

Mark Brock turned out to be a tall, strongly built, dark man with arresting green eyes and profoundly black, thick hair spilling down his head to his shoulders, covering his arms and sprouting through the exposed parts of his shirt. His whole being exuded a sense of natural authority and power without the taint of intimidation. His movements were as fluid as those of a tiger, his grip firm and his smile devastating.

"Hi, I'm Mark," he said as she entered, reaching out a hand which Megan took. She flinched—Mark's unexpected strength had caught her off guard. Between the spell of his dancing eyes and the power in his hands she felt paralyzed. Sensing this, Mark smiled and gently let go her hand while softening the intensity of his glance. Megan stared at him, breathing hard for a few moments before the spectacle of her rudeness flashed across her. She blushed.

"I'm Megan," she answered smoothly, regaining her poise, moving past him toward her locker at the same time.

Zack appeared to be absorbed with contemplating his tea. Megan ignored him as she stuffed her coat into her locker.

Mark smiled.

"I met Zack earlier this morning," he said affably as Megan poured out some coffee and sat down at the table, trying hard not to stare at him. Mark, on his part, kept his glance and tone of voice neutral as though aware of its effect on her. She gradually relaxed and felt a sense of normalcy returning to her thoughts.

"He's told me a lot about you," he continued.

Megan looked up sharply with a dangerous gleam in her eyes in spite of herself.

"I hope it was all *good*," she said, with an emphasis that caused Zack to suddenly long for the fresh air outside.

"Of course it was," rejoined Mark and the cloud vanished from her face.

"Absolutely," muttered Zack.

Megan shrugged her shoulders indifferently although her emotions were boiling inside.

Rolla and Kip came in together, shuffled off their coats and then stared in surprise at Mark's unfamiliar face.

"This is the new guy," said Zack, by way of introduction. "Mark, meet Kip and Rolla."

Kip and Rolla both shook hands with Mark and headed for their lockers. Kip paused long enough to whisper to Megan, "What happened to Lisa?"

His face fell as she slowly shook her head.

He muttered something darkly and went to his locker.

As Kip and Rolla sat down, Drak and Shawn came through the door, stopping in surprise as they caught sight of Mark.

"Mark, this is Drak and Shawn," announced Megan before Zack could react.

Zack gave Megan an enigmatic glance, stood up from the table and went over to the new arrivals, saying something to them in a low voice. Their faces clouded over and they shook their heads disgustedly. Zack came back to his chair and sat down.

After these first introductions, Mark sat quietly in his chair, turning over the pages of a book he was reading. Megan happened to glance at it and her eyes widened slightly. Its white dust jacket looked as though it were absolutely blank. Pure white without a mark on its surface.

"Is this the new person?"

All of them looked up, startled, their animated conversations frozen into silence. Donna stood in the doorway to the break room—*how was it they hadn't heard her coming?*—looking them over disdainfully.

Enjoys showing off her power, doesn't she? thought Megan.

She lingered in the doorway instead of immediately leaving as she usually did. Megan looked at her in surprise and then growing concern at the expression on her face. *Who or what is she staring at so darkly?* she wondered.

It wasn't until a few seconds later she realized that *Mark* was the focus of her displeasure. Megan was puzzled for a moment and suddenly realized *he had not taken the slightest notice of her dramatic entrance.* He remained absorbed in his book, never looking up from it once.

She can't reach him, flashed through Megan's mind.

Donna's eyes narrowed and she took a heavy step into the room. The others instinctively shrank back into their seats but she paid them no attention: she only had eyes for Mark. Mark only had eyes for his book—he still showed no sign he had seen her.

Megan shot Donna a quick glance and trembled. It was obvious she wasn't going to put up with this much longer.

She sucked in her breath with a venomous hiss, as though gathering herself to spring and then harshly grated out, "Hel*lo?*" her voice echoing off the walls.

Mark looked up languidly at the sound and stared straight into her eyes.

There was not an ounce of fear in his.

"Did you need something?" he asked, blandly.

Some of the fire died in her eyes at the sound of his voice. Although he was perfectly relaxed and spoke quietly, his voice had an embedded steely sharpness that completely neutralized her poison. She found herself hesitating. That gave her pause.

Furious for showing a sign of weakness in front of witnesses, she suddenly spat out coldly, "I'm your new supervisor."

Mark smiled.

"Pleased to meet you, Donna. My name is Mark," and with that he went back to his book amidst the stunned silence that descended on the room.

For a moment, Donna was nonplussed but she quickly recovered herself, clenching her hands tight enough to drive the color from her knuckles. Her neck mottled and her face flushed as she turned her anger on the others sitting at the table.

"I *think* it's after eight-twenty," she snarled.

They quickly pushed their chairs back from the table, rose and walked down the hallway toward the counter area. All except Mark. He stood up as they left, stretched and looked straight at her. She blinked.

"You planning on working with us today?" she snapped out rudely.

"Certainly," replied Mark amiably.

"Well then I suggest you get out to the counter!" she ordered in a louder voice.

"I'd love to," replied Mark, unruffled. "However, in order for me to do that you have to issue me a cash fund and a set of keys—I assume you already have them ready with the receipts for my signature?—and assign me to a station."

She stared at him in amazement. He continued in the same, affable tone of voice:

"You *could* send me outside instead—but I haven't been certified on your drive test course and we'd have to wait for a Tech to find the time to do that."

She paled and took a deep breath but merely exhaled hard and replied, "Follow me!"

She turned away and left the room. Mark slipped his book into a locker and followed her through the counter area into her office, shutting the door behind him.

Megan, Zack, and the rest of the counter staff stared after them with open mouths. Zack was the first to recover and he turned back to his station, punching the **CALL NEXT** button. The monotonous voice immediately summoned the next customer.

"How did he get away with that?" breathed Megan, still in shock.

"With what?" asked Zack, distracted, watching the lobby for signs of his customer.

"He called her by her first name. *No* one ever does that. If one of us—" but Zack cut her off impatiently with a wave of his hand.

"Yeah yeah—if one of us did it we'd be pulverized. But he wasn't, so just deal with it."

Megan flushed angrily.

"Whose side are you on, anyway?" she hissed.

Zack shrugged his shoulders and attended to the customer who had just reached his station. Megan gritted her teeth in frustration and turned back to her station, angrily punching her **CALL NEXT** button.

About an hour later, the door to the office opened. Donna stood in the doorway, her face masked in shadow by the bright light behind her, and called out, "Zack!"

She vanished into her office. Zack sighed, finished with his customer and locked down his station. He pushed back his chair and headed to her office.

"Ready for you," Donna announced curtly as he entered and busied herself with some paperwork on her desk, ignoring him. Zack looked around and saw Mark sitting in one of the chairs with an air of quiet amusement—*amusement?*—dancing in his eyes.

"You got a few minutes?" asked Zack, out of habit.

"Sure," replied Mark with a grin.

"Come into the checkout room."

They walked out of the office to the checkout room, Zack pushing the door shut behind him as they entered.

"I take it this is my briefing?" asked Mark, still grinning.

"Yeah. You worked for the agency long?"

"Ten years."

"I guess we can skip most of the bullshit then," said Zack.

Mark laughed.

"Do you have any questions?" Zack continued.

"Only the usual *'where do I hang up my coat?'* and things like that."

Zack nodded.

"She gave you your keys and cash drawer already?"

"Yeah. She wants me to work station three today."

Zack rolled his eyes.

"You'll *love* that one. First-time ID cards."

Mark smiled.

"I can deal with it."

"You already saw the break room. The fridge is there, hot water spout, coffee pot. Just don't leave any food out unless you want to share it with the rodents."

Mark laughed again. "Some things are the same wherever you go," he observed.

Zack nodded.

"The locker you picked out okay?"

Mark shrugged.

"I've got no beef with it."

Zack paused. He felt exhausted, as though he had been swimming against a strong current or climbing an endless flight of stairs. He tried to puzzle out the reason for this, then gave up and continued.

"Have you heard anything about—about our supervisor?"

"You mean Donna?"

Zack winced as though expecting an explosion.

"Nothing really," continued Mark. "I doubt I'd care if I did."

That was not what Zack expected to hear and it threw him off his stride.

"Nothing at *all?*" he asked, disbelievingly.

"No," replied Mark evenly.

"Really?"

"*Really.*"

Zack wasn't quite sure how to proceed beyond this point. He was silent for a few minutes before saying, "So, you haven't heard about her reputation or the things that have happened here—?" but Mark interrupted him smoothly.

"I *may* have but I ignore things like that. I don't deal with other people's opinions. I like to form mine for myself."

He said this politely but Zack reddened as though rebuked. He felt himself falling into sullenness and struggled against it.

"I think you should at least be aware of what you're getting into," he began but again Mark silenced him.

"I know enough to be able to deal with anything that might come up," he said. "I'm able to take my own actions to defend myself if I have to."

A wave of anger washed over Zack again. As he fought it down successfully, he suddenly realized what he was doing: he was fighting to assert himself—*as though he had lost control of the situation and was desperate to get it back*. He instantly felt ashamed for thinking in those terms: he wasn't interested in control. *Or had his position as Shop Steward blinded him to a need he didn't know he had?*

Regardless, he knew Mark would not surrender control of the situation to him. There was nothing he could do but accept it. He struggled to breathe for few moments—*why had he been holding his breath?*—and finally calmed himself down to the point where his voice wouldn't betray his feelings.

Mark took no notice.

"Well," said Zack at last, heavily, "You know that if you need anything I'm available for you," and forced himself to stand up and stretch. Mark followed suit.

"I really appreciate the offer. I understand why you're making it—I have no problem with that. But I can assure you that I'll be able to handle myself just fine. If I *do* run into something I can't handle I'll definitely let you know."

At this, Zack relaxed. Although Mark had not changed his tone of voice there was an undercurrent of apology running through the last speech that calmed his raw nerves. He held out his hand and Mark shook it without breaking his fingers.

"Well—I had to say it and now I've said it," said Zack.

Mark smiled.

"It's okay," and with that he gave Zack a reassuring grip on the shoulder, opened the door and glided over to station three. He logged in, pressed the **CALL NEXT** button and began waiting on customers.

3

AT DAGGERS DRAWN

"Bullshit!"

Everyone at the counter and in the lobby instinctively turned toward the source of the ugly sound. The staff tensed, knowing what was coming. A sudden verbal explosion out of nowhere usually was the prelude to a *'difficult customer incident.'*

The lobby went quiet. The other customers at the counter tried to turn their heads to observe the shouter without being obvious about it. Megan didn't have to look; she was familiar with this person and his monthly visits to the office.

At least it isn't my turn this time, she smiled grimly. Kip was the victim on the block today—his face was already red and his voice mangled his words as he tried to keep calm and deal with the customer. The customer, for his part, seemed delighted in his immunity from retaliation, putting in a taunting barb whenever he could. Kip's attempts to defuse the situation only goaded him further.

Kip's voice was too low for her to catch the words but it was obvious the stress was taking a toll. The customer mouthed Kip's words with twisted exaggeration, sticking his tongue out derisively as he did so.

"*Leave?*" he screamed, in response to Kip. "**Leave?** *You* can't make me leave! I'm tired of being —d around by you jerks! I'm *not* leaving until I get my god-damned driver license!" his voice rising to a traumatic screech.

Kip blinked and stepped back from his station to the delight of the customer who lunged forward in response. Exclamations of alarm and disgust erupted throughout the lobby. A child started to bawl. The customer turned around and glared threateningly at the crowd. His face was covered with stubble, his skin smeared black with grime, his clothes hanging in tatters on his emaciated frame. The stench of his unwashed body wafted forward with every movement. His eyes were blazing.

"Call the police! I *dare* you! Call them!!" and he turned back, pounding on the counter with both fists.

Megan was reaching for the alarm switch when a voice spoke behind her.

"What's *his* beef?"

Megan whirled. It was Mark.

He was as calm and cool as ever. His muscles were a little more taut than normal and his eyes were harder but those were the only visible signs of his concern.

"It's Mr. Davis," replied Megan.

"What's *his* problem?" asked Mark again.

"He's got a suspension for child-support and a string of unpaid fines. He's homeless and has some mental issues—sometimes he doesn't take his meds. He usually shows up to

36

scream at us about once a month—but I've never seen him this bad..."

Mark was already moving toward Kip's station.

Megan had forgotten her customer in the heat of the action but the customer was just as riveted as she was on the unfolding drama. She glanced at him and he smiled, putting his finger to his lips. She smiled back and they both watched—her hand still within reach of the switch.

"Who the f— are *you* supposed to be? Captain Dickhead coming to the rescue?" was Mr. Davis's greeting to Mark.

Mark remained silent, his face absolutely devoid of expression. Mr. Davis evidently did not take this lack of response well and launched a new verbal attack.

"What's the deal? Are you," he sneered, jabbing his finger at Kip, "this guy's running dog or something? He's too chickenshit to throw his own punches so he calls *you* in? F— that. I can take *both* of you on—" and he took up a classic boxer's stance, both fists at the ready.

Mark spoke to him and Mr. Davis's torrent of words instantly ceased; he slowly lowered his hands to his sides. Mark's voice was even less audible than Kip's—yet Mr. Davis did not interrupt him while he was talking and listened intently. It reminded Megan of a dog with its ears forward, its nose following the rise and fall of its master's voice. The vision was so intensely real she started and looked sharply in Mark's direction as if to confirm what she saw—but the image vanished and did not reappear.

"What's going on here?" grated a familiar voice from across the lobby.

Oh my gawd, thought Megan, as Donna strode over to Kip's station. *She is going to totally screw this up!* Kip saw her approaching and stepped back up to his station, trying to get Mark's attention. Mark did not notice and continued talking to Mr. Davis. Donna walked up and shouldered him aside, catching him completely unawares, nearly knocking him over. As he fought to regain his balance, Megan trembled at the sudden change in his eyes: *the mask had slipped for a moment.* He instantly regained control of himself and turned his full attention to Donna.

Donna was in fine form—screaming even louder than Mr. Davis had. Mr. Davis had stepped back from the counter, amazed. However, he was far from intimidated. He looked like a furious horse with its ears flattened to its skull. Megan saw the fire in his eyes ignite; she shivered as she saw him tighten his jaw and muscles. *He's getting ready to explode*, she thought.

"How many times is it going to take for you get it? *You are suspended!* You've got to pay your fines and your child support or you aren't getting anything! Get over it! Get your worthless, reeking carcass out of my office or I'll have you thrown—"

Megan closed her eyes, not wanting to witness the outcome. She opened them quickly, staring wildly, when Donna's rant suddenly cut off in mid-sentence. Megan could not believe her eyes: Mark, his hand firmly gripping Donna's shoulder, had spun her around to face him. She was white to the lips and shaking but made no move to dislodge his hand, remaining silent while he said, loud enough for at least the counter staff to hear:

"*You* need to go back into your office, shut the door and chill out. I've got this situation under control and I'd appreciate you not screwing it up anymore than you already have. If *I* need your assistance, I'll ask you for it. **Get out of here!**"

Megan watched, transfixed with horror, as Donna slipped out from Mark's grip and stared at him, her lips twitching silently. Suddenly, her face flushed and she ran from the lobby back into her office, slamming the door behind her.

It sounded like a cannon shot.

Mark then turned to Mr. Davis who was just as shocked as the other witnesses to this scene.

"I apologize for that, Mr. Davis," said Mark.

Mr. Davis stared at him incredulously.

"Why don't you step over here," said Mark, making his way to the end station, "And let me see what I can do to help you."

Mr. Davis swallowed hard, blinked and followed him to the end station quietly, the memory of his threatening demeanor in shreds. Amidst a deathly silence, he sat down and engaged in a quiet conversation with Mark.

The entire lobby breathed a collective sigh of relief and the usual noise of muted chatter returned. The counter staff looked at each other in amazement as did their customers. Megan took a deep breath and finished her transaction. Her customer was so stunned he almost walked off without his change.

A few minutes later, Mr. Davis rose from his chair, walked quietly over to Kip's station and said to him, in a firm, steady voice:

"I apologize for going off at you, sir. I didn't mean to take it out on you."

Kip swallowed hard but gave him a nod of assurance and, with that, Mr. Davis turned away and walked out of the lobby. As the doors shut behind him someone in the rows started clapping and a brief round of applause swept the room. Mark did not acknowledge it. His face dark, he waved off Kip's thanks and headed for the office.

Megan tried hard not to listen when he opened the door but there was nothing to hear. The door shut and all was back to normal.

For now, she thought.

It was too cold and wet even for Zack to walk outside after work. The gusting wind twisting and pulling the leafless branches did not make it any more inviting. He and Megan drove to a sandwich shop and ordered some food and coffee. The seats were the usual uncomfortable hard plastic and the ambiance was hardly conducive to prolonged dining—but both of them were too involved in their conversation to notice.

"You're kidding! He did it *again?*" said Zack, his eyes wide from Megan's spirited description of Mark's encounter with Mr. Davis.

"Yeah," nodded Megan, biting into her sandwich, "and he got away with it again, too."

Zack shook his head in disbelief.

"I don't believe this guy. I mean, *I* try not to let her push me around and all that but that's nothing compared to what he's doing. He's—he's *taming* her!"

Megan's eyes narrowed.

"Let's see what happens tomorrow."

"Probably nothing," said Zack thoughtfully. "What did she do after he '*faced*' her at the counter?"

Megan swallowed another bite of her sandwich.

"Walked into her office, slammed the door and didn't come out for the rest of the day."

Zack laughed bitterly.

"That's what she did the other two times," he remarked. "You're right. It looks like he's getting off free on this one like last time."

"I don't think so," said Megan, reaching for her drink. "Like you said, you can only push so much before it recoils."

Zack nodded his head, absently.

"Unless this is part of the righting process," he replied. Then he looked up at her sharply as though suddenly realizing what she had said.

"You talking about *balance?*" he queried, suspiciously

"Yeah. Balance," said Megan flatly.

Zack looked at her strangely. Megan felt herself getting uncomfortable.

"What?" she asked at last, a touch of annoyance in her voice.

"I didn't think you took it seriously," he responded, slowly.

Megan tossed her head and grabbed another bite.

"You'd be surprised what I take seriously."

Zack muttered something and stared at his coffee cup but his eyes focused inward, far away from the hard table in the sandwich shop.

"Looks like he's still with us," said Zack as they sat down for lunch.

"Yeah," nodded Drak.

"I can't believe he did that, yesterday," said Shawn. "That had to have taken some serious balls."

Drak rolled his eyes.

"*I'm* more amazed that he got through to Mr. Davis. Do you know," he continued, turning to Zack, "they've actually dealt with him down at HQ and *they* threw him out too? *Twice!* And here Mark goes and just says some magic words and he walks out of here like a lamb!"

Drak shook his head in amazement.

"She didn't call him in the office or anything this morning?" asked Zack.

"Nah," said Drak.

"Well," said Shawn, washing his cup out in the sink and putting it on the rack, "I'm glad he's on *our* team. Things are a lot better around here since he showed up."

He put on his coat, grabbed his clipboard and headed outside.

"Amen to that," said Drak.

Megan nodded in agreement.

"I wonder how in the hell he does it," added Drak, as if to himself.

"Probably uses something out of that book he's always reading," said Zack as he rose, washed off his plate and poured a glass of water.

"It wouldn't surprise me," said Megan.

"That must be some book," said Drak. "He's *always* reading it. If he's not out doing drives or working the counter he's back here reading that book. Really strange."

"Anyone know the name of that book?" asked Zack.

There was a pause.

"No," said Megan finally. The others shrugged their shoulders.

"I think it's one of those '*trick picture*' books," said Drak.

"Trick picture books?" repeated Megan with a laugh.

"Yeah. You know—those books that came out in the early 80s that had those hidden pictures? Like if you looked at them just right they'd turn into a three-dimensional image or something like that?"

Megan snapped her fingers.

"*I* remember those! Hated those damn things."

"Why?" asked Drak.

Megan ran her fingers through her hair, irritably.

"I never could get them to work for me. Everyone was always oohing and aahing about what they were seeing—but I never could see anything. Treated me like I was some kind of moron 'cause I couldn't '*get it*.'"

Her face flushed at the memory. She took a swallow of her drink.

"Same here," said Zack. "They just looked like weird pictures to me."

"I think it was a scam," said Megan through gritted teeth.

"No," said Drak, "*I* saw something. Not every time, but sometimes."

Megan reddened and looked down at the table.

"Well *I* never did," she muttered defensively.

Drak, glanced at his watch, then at the clock, sighed, pushed back his chair and headed toward the counter.

"How is everyone?" came a voice from the door a few minutes later.

"Yo Mark," they responded as he made his way into the break room. He smiled and went up to his locker. He opened it, reached inside, pulled out a sandwich along with the book— the book that he was never without except when on duty—and sat down at the table.

Megan could never remember what the book looked like but she always recognized it as soon as she saw it. It was a thick, hardback book, shaped like a ledger with a white dust jacket. At least that's how Megan thought of it: a rectangle. She found it hard to keep her eyes off it although there was no reason for her fascination: the dust cover was white without a picture or title.

No, she thought, *that's not quite right*. There *was* a title or some kind of lettering on the front cover but she could never make it out. The best description of her impression was that it was a bright silver font or some equally mismatched color that made it impossible to read from a distance. *It could have something to do with the glare too*, she thought. Every time she tried to look at it closely, she found herself squinting as though she were looking at an intense, bright light.

Her eyes started aching as she made another attempt at deciphering the title. She forced herself to turn away only to find her vision clouded with dark spots—as though she actually *had* looked straight into a bright light.

Megan rubbed her eyes instinctively and suddenly noticed that Zack was doing the same thing. She quickly looked over at Mark but Mark had shifted position so his arms blocked the cover from view. Megan looked at Zack and they both shrugged.

Mark continued to read and eat his sandwich in silence while Zack and Megan conversed in low tones. They knew Mark enough by now to know he was not being intentionally rude; he was friendly and polite if he asked any questions when reading. But for some reason it took a lot of courage to make the first move in talking to him. All of the staff tended to leave him undisturbed during his lunches and breaks.

Although everyone was dying to find out, none of them would have dreamed of asking about the incident with Mr. Davis. They were even less disposed to ask (but more interested to know) if there had been any backlash from Donna over their confrontation.

A heavy footstep sounded at the door. And a familiar voice.

"Everyone okay?"

Dead silence fell.

It was Donna.

Her surprise visits to the break room had dwindled to the point that it was rare to see her figure in the doorway. It was even rarer to see her sitting at the table since she now tended to eat her lunch and take her breaks in her office. Although she was still able to create instant silence on entry, her air of arrogant disdain had been replaced by wariness and distrust.

Like a lion-tamer who suspects she is a future victim, always on her guard even with the whip in her hand.

As usual, Mark did not even look up from his reading or see her as she entered. Megan saw her go pale and bite her lip, her eyes fixed on Mark with virulent intensity. Megan blinked and the moment was gone. Donna's color returned to normal and she walked in quietly, heading for the hot water dispenser, her cup in her hand.

Her route to the sink took her past Mark's chair. She drew her water, tore open a tea bag and placed it in her cup. As she turned to go, her eyes passed over Mark. She suddenly stiffened, her eyes dilating and her teeth clenching with a muted hiss. She quietly put the cup down next to the drain board.

Alarmed, Megan touched Zack's hand as she watched Donna walk up stealthily behind Mark, slowly reach over his shoulder and then suddenly snatch the book right out of his hands. An expression of vicious triumph bloated her face as she quickened her pace toward the door, clutching the book under her arm, abandoning her teacup in her hurry.

Mark was instantly on his feet, his air of languid indifference gone.

"Ex*cuse* me?" he asked.

Donna stopped dead in her tracks as though she'd run into a wall—the shock visibly rippled through her body. Slowly she turned around, as though forced, breathing hard, until she was facing Mark with defiance blazing in her eyes, gripping the book with white fingers.

"Did I say you could take my book?"

His voice was as polite as ever but there was a subtle change in its usual timbre that demanded respect and attention. Donna stared at him without answering.

"Why are you taking my book?"

She suddenly came to life, flushed red and snapped out, "You can't have that book in here. It's inappropriate material! I'm keeping it in my office until the end of the day. Then you can take it home and never bring it back here again!"

She tried to turn to go but halted immediately. Despite her muscles and body visibly straining to continue, she could not move from her spot. Sweat broke out on her face and she breathed shallowly through clenched teeth as she glared at him.

"What do you mean by *'inappropriate material'*, if I may ask?"

She tried, with difficulty, to answer without screaming.

"It's *pornography!*" she snarled. "That's not allowed here."

Mark stepped back. His eyes widened, his eyebrows rose and he suddenly burst into laughter, collapsing into his chair with mirth.

"Pornography? Oh *please*—" and his laughter overcame him again. Megan and Zack did not laugh. Their eyes were riveted on Donna's face which slowly passed from white, to red and finally to purple.

"Yes, pornography! You know you can't bring that stuff to work! You're lucky I'm not reporting you to Lilly!"

Again, she tried to go but still could not budge from where she stood. She began to make strange, strangled sounds like an animal caught in the blades of a steel trap.

"Zack?" asked Mark, politely. Zack started and looked at him.

"Do *you* see anything pornographic in my book?"

Zack, as though in a trance, got up and walked over to Donna, taking the book from her suddenly nerveless hands. He flipped through the pages. He stopped a couple of times and narrowed his eyes, but resumed turning pages until he shrugged his shoulders and handed the book to Mark.

"No," he replied flatly, handing the book to Mark.

"Megan? Would you mind looking?" asked Mark, handing her the book.

Megan did not reach out for it immediately because she was struck by the look on Zack's face. He was staring intently at Mark but she could not decipher his expression. She shook her head, took the book and flipped through the pages with a growing expression of bewilderment.

"There's nothing but blank pages," she reported, baffled.

Donna, as though suddenly released from bondage, darted forward, grabbed the book from her and started whipping furiously through the pages—grimly at first, then hesitantly and then in shocked amazement.

"They're blank," she whispered, loud enough for the others to hear. "They're all blank," she repeated. She suddenly looked up at them, fear and anger chasing themselves across her face.

"I know I saw *something!*" she began to wail, then faltered as she saw the unanimous expression of doubt on their faces. She put the book down on the table and slowly backed away, staring at Mark the whole time. Mark's glance was no less intense as he followed her; for a moment, Megan felt her eyes ache again as though a sunbeam had flashed across her vision. Donna suddenly turned, walked toward the door, then broke into a run, her footsteps fading away on the hallway tiles.

Mark smiled, picked up the book and put it in his locker. Megan looked at Zack and shrugged her shoulders. Zack muttered something inaudible, lowered his eyes and left the room, heading back to the counter.

Megan walked over to the drain board, picked up the forgotten teacup, started to walk out to the counter with it— then thought better of it and poured it out into the sink, rinsed it and put it into the drying rack.

Later that afternoon, Rolla came in from outside and sat down at the table with a sigh of relief. Zack joined her shortly afterward. Then Mark came walking in.

"Hi guys," he said.

They nodded and he walked over to his locker. He opened the door, reached inside and suddenly froze. A strange look came into his face. He groped with his hand, bent down and peered inside the locker. He snapped upright and sprinted down the hall.

Rolla and Zack looked at each other wonderingly.

Immediately they heard the sound of footsteps returning. Footsteps and voices. At the sound of one of the voices they both tensed: Donna was approaching. She was furious.

"Who the hell do you think you are, coming into *my* office and taking things off of *my* desk? Where do you get off? My office is *my* office and you don't have any business—"

Mark came in carrying his book, Donna right at his heels like a dog harrying a cat. As they entered the break room Mark suddenly spun around to face her, forcing her to skid to avoid running into him. All of them were appalled at the expression on his face: this time the mask hadn't merely slipped—*it had been torn off.*

"You listen to me," said Mark, his voice cold enough to chill the blood. His eyes blazed with an intensity of anger that not even Donna could withstand. She backed up from him, terrified.

"Let me give you a valuable piece of advice," he continued, his speech precise and clipped. "Stealing this out of my locker is so far out of line that you've got nothing to say about *me* going in and retrieving it off of your desk. *You stole this! You have no right to it!*"

He paused, breathing hard.

"This isn't something you just casually pick up and browse through without permission," he continued. "You don't know what you're doing—" and he stopped again for a moment.

She stared at him, trembling.

"Now," he continued in a slightly less intense tone of voice, "I can't stop you from killing yourself if you have that bad of a death wish. You can blow me off if you have *that* much faith in your arrogance—but I still need to say this to clear my conscience: do *not* read this book alone. It's dangerous. Reading it in your office with the door closed is suicidal."

He paused for a moment to let this sink in.

"You're stepping into something way too deep for you to swim in. You don't have a clue what you're getting into. Don't ever touch my book again! If you do, *I'm not going to be responsible for what happens to you!*"

Donna blanched. Then turned purple with anger.

"You want to continue this conversation we'll do it in Lilly's office!" Mark stated before she could open her mouth. He leaned back against his locker, his arms crossed over his chest.

Donna ground her teeth so hard it was audible. Zack winced at the sound.

"*You* are in no position to take risks," added Mark, significantly. With that, Donna drew herself up, turned around and stalked out of the room down the hallway. Megan came in immediately afterward.

"Man!" she breathed, looking behind her. "If looks could kill she'd have wiped out the whole lobby!"

Mark suddenly regained his poise and restored his veil of inscrutability. *And yet*, thought Megan, *he wasn't quite the same as he was before*. Something new was in his eyes. *Sadness? Grief?* The thought amazed her but she had no time to consider it. Mark looked up and saw them staring at him.

He flushed red but it wasn't anger.

"I'm sorry you guys," he said. "I didn't mean to drag you all into this," and he sat down at the table with a weariness Megan had never seen in him before. He sunk his head into his hands and remained motionless for a few moments.

Zack stayed in his seat at the table, staring at Mark with a grim face. Megan and Rolla traded glances. Rolla quickly rinsed out her cup and left. Megan hesitated, then followed her out. She cast back a glance full of concern but neither Zack nor Mark acknowledged it.

Mark finally stirred and raised his face to discover Zack, still sitting at the table, staring at him sternly.

Mark just looked at him for a moment.

"Well?" he asked, in response to his look.

"Those pages didn't look blank to *me*," said Zack coldly.

Mark's expression changed instantly and he regarded Zack with a different, almost *intimate* attitude—as though they were conspirators sharing a joint secret. He smiled. Zack did not respond.

"You mean you can see something on those pages?" Mark asked, curiously.

48

"Yes."

Mark phrased his next question cautiously.

"What do you see?"

Zack shrugged.

"Just pictures. I can't make out what they are but I know they're there. They're *not* pornographic, whatever they are."

"Good so far," said Mark encouragingly. "Anything else?"

Zack's eyes gleamed for a moment in surprise at Mark's tone of voice.

"They—they remind me of those hidden picture books, those ones from the 80s, remember? The ones that would look three-dimensional—" but Mark interrupted him with a smile.

"Ah. I had forgotten about those. Interesting. And it makes sense."

Mark leaned back in his chair, locking his hands behind his neck, relaxing with an attitude that Zack found troubling. *It was as though Mark had temporarily laid aside his power.* Zack leaned back in his chair as well.

"I'm afraid I owe you an apology," began Mark. "I didn't take you as seriously as you deserved to be. It's what I get for being an elitist."

Zack was completely at a loss.

"Elitist?" he repeated.

"Well—it's like you get so used to being the only enlightened person in the room you start to make the mistake of thinking everyone else is an idiot. Kind of puts the lie to my own ego as it were. I shouldn't have fallen into that trap."

Zack shook his head, baffled.

"I don't understand what you're saying."

"You understand enough of it, though," said Mark reassuringly. "And you understand more of it than the others."

Zack tried to work this through and gave up with a sigh.

"What is the thing about those pictures in that book? Are you saying that only certain people can see things in it? Depending on how '*enlightened*' they are?"

Mark laughed.

"No—not quite. What you see depends not so much on whether you are *'enlightened'* but on who you are," he said, "Or rather, how you choose to see things," he added enigmatically in a lower tone, staring at the cover of the book.

"What *is* that book?" Zack asked suddenly. Mark looked up.

"What do you mean?"

"What is it called?"

"You can't read the title?" asked Mark, holding up the cover with a smile.

Zack looked at it closely.

"I can see *something* on the dust jacket," he said, finally. "I can't make it out though—the light is bad in here or something," and he rubbed his eyes.

Mark nodded as though he had expected this.

"They don't look like English letters to me," Zack added.

"They're not," said Mark.

"Well, what *is* the title?" asked Zack after a pause.

"***Isorropia***," Mark replied.

There was not a flicker of recognition in Zack's eyes at this word.

"Look it up on the internet," said Mark, his mask slipping into place once more. "It's Greek."

Zack said nothing.

Mark put the book back in his locker, fished around inside, pulled out a padlock and secured the door, pocketing the key.

They both stood up and silently made their way to the counter.

Megan was waiting for Zack in the parking lot that evening. He walked out of the door, saw Megan, and slowly walked toward her. After a few minutes, Mark emerged and quickly made his way to his car. Zack appeared to be too preoccupied with his thoughts to notice him as he passed. Mark smiled at Megan and said, "Good night!" cheerfully as he crossed the lot toward his spot.

Megan nodded and stared after him gravely. Zack reached her side a few moments later and stopped, following Mark's departure with his eyes. He said nothing.

Mark climbed into his immaculate machine, fired up the engine and drove out of the parking lot, his taillights fading into the darkness.

Silence fell. It grew colder.

With a sigh, Megan drew her coat closer and turned to go.

"Megan?" asked Zack suddenly; she gave a start. She hadn't realized he was standing next to her.

"Yes?" she answered.

"Can we have dinner, tonight?"

Megan clenched her fists to hide her emotion.

"Are you *serious?*" she responded, instantly gritting her teeth painfully. *I didn't mean to say that out loud!* rang through her head.

"Yes," said Zack, slowly, "yes, I guess I *am* serious."

"You mean right *now?*" she asked, looking at herself. "I'm— I'm not really dressed to go out."

"You won't need to dress up," said Zack. "We can eat at my place," and he turned and walked away, as though assuming she'd decline.

Megan blushed and her eyes glowed. She recovered herself, ran and caught up to him quickly, sensing his departure.

She somehow managed to link arms with him without fainting or doing something equally ridiculous and preserved her semblance of calm, slowing the rapid pulse of her heart.

"Okay," she whispered.

Zack smiled.

4

SURRENDER

"Zack?"

"Yes?" he replied.

His expression, obscured in the darkness beyond the candlelight, was unreadable.

Megan frowned slightly but by this time, her internal glow had so permeated her soul that nothing could quench it. Try as she might she couldn't shake off the dreamy contentment that possessed her—the momentary frustration at not being able to see his face passed off quickly.

"Since when did you know how to cook?"

Zack looked up from his plate, the twin candle flames glinting in his eyes and laughed.

"Don't you remember?" he asked, playfully. "I was in the Air Force as a cook for years."

She laughed in her turn and trimmed off another piece of lasagna with her fork.

"I didn't forget that," she answered demurely, "but don't try and tell me that they cook like this in the Air Force."

His smile was just visible.

"I've been cooking since I was about ten."

"*Ten?*" she repeated, not believing it. She speared the trimmed piece with her fork and swallowed it.

"Yeah," he affirmed, capturing a piece of salad. "Started off with tuna casserole and worked my way up to the hard stuff like chocolate cakes by the time I was twelve."

She laughed again.

"And here I thought I knew you all this time," she said, archly.

"It goes both ways," he responded. She looked up at him.

"What do you mean?" she asked, puzzled.

He sipped some of his wine.

"I thought I knew me all this time too."

She thought this over for a moment, felt a chill of resentment, then surrendered to the glow again.

"I don't understand," she said, half to herself, but still smiling.

"That makes two of us," was the response.

He sighed.

"Want any more?" he asked, noticing she made no further attacks on her plate.

She nodded.

"I'm good," she said.

Zack pushed back his chair and stood up, gathering his dishes together. Megan watched him for a moment, then, realizing what he was doing, stood up from the table herself.

"You need any help?" she asked.

Zack smiled.

"No—no," he replied, carrying his dishes to the sink.

"You sure?" she called out to him.

He laughed again.

"I'm not afraid of doing dishes."

She raised her eyebrows but only because he wasn't in the dining room. She gathered her dishes and carried them to the sink, passing him on the way in to the kitchen. Between the two of them they soon had the table cleared and the cloth put away, leaving only the candles burning in their holders.

"Shall I blow these out?" asked Megan.

"Nah," replied Zack, passing into the kitchen again. "Just take them into the living room and put them on the coffee table."

This can't be happening, thought Megan.

She carefully moved the candles, one at a time, to the coffee table in the living room and sat down on the couch with a sigh of pleasure. She could hear Zack fossicking around in the kitchen with the dishes; her eyes danced as she envisioned him at the sink, cleaning and scrubbing. She leaned back and closed her eyes. Aside from the candles, the room was in darkness. The visible world ended just beyond the coffee table.

"You sure you don't need my help?" she called out at one point.

"I'm okay," responded Zack from the kitchen.

"You want some coffee or tea or anything?" he asked as the dishwasher began its humming.

"Tea would be nice if you have herbal," she responded, her heart suddenly pounding hard.

A clatter of cups and saucers followed. Then silence except for the busy sounds of the dishwasher until the truculent teakettle whistle sounded. It ceased instantly and there was a sound of water pouring. Then footsteps approaching.

Megan bit her lip. *Let's see where he sits.*

Zack came in carrying a tray with a teapot, two cups, a basket, a jug of cream and a bowl of sugar. He carefully set the tray down from the opposite side of the table and poured out the water. The darkness hid the look of disappointment on

Megan's face. Surrendering to the weariness suddenly flowing through her body, she slumped back in her seat, numbed.

"Got all kinds of herbal here," he said cheerfully, indicating the basket bristling with tea bags. Megan leaned forward listlessly and looked through them, selected a peppermint bag and dropped it into her hot water, swirling the bag as she did so. Zack already had a tea bag in his cup and poured some cream in with the water. Megan closed her eyes for a moment—and then opened them wide as she felt something settle on the couch next to her.

My gawd, her thoughts raced. *He **did** sit here.*

Her expression passed from disappointment to awe.

As Zack picked up his cup, Megan leaned forward for hers, slightly shifting her position so she wound up closer to him. She could feel the glow pouring into her face again and was very grateful for the darkness. She could hardly breathe, her heartbeat thundering in her ears.

Zack unconsciously shifted himself closer to her in response. She exhaled with a sigh and leaned back, almost spilling her tea. She caught herself in time and glanced at him guiltily but he was staring straight ahead into the darkness.

They sat there for a few minutes, savoring the warmth in their cups and the warmth from each other.

"What a strange day," said Megan, unaware she was saying it out loud. She managed not to gasp as she realized her mistake but Zack simply responded with, "No kidding."

They sat for a few minutes more, sipping their tea.

"What happened with Mark and Donna this afternoon?" asked Zack suddenly.

"What do you mean?" asked Megan.

"Well I guess she stole his book out of his locker while he was out on drives. He came in to the break room, saw it was gone and dashed out front. He came right back with the book and she was right behind him, screaming something about him taking things off of her desk—"

Megan frowned.

"So *that's* what that was all about," she said.

"What did he do out there?" asked Zack.

Megan shook her head.

"I don't remember her taking the book into her office. First thing I saw was when he ran out of the hallway over to her office door. Her shade was drawn, like always and he tried to look through the slats—I guess he wanted to see what she was doing or something."

"Well *then* what?" prodded Zack.

Megan drank some of her tea.

"He said something—sounded like '*fool*'—and went inside."

"Just '*went inside*'?" Zack repeated, as though not convinced.

Megan knitted her brows as if doubting her memory.

"No—he pushed it open so hard I think he left a dent in her wall. He ran over to her, pulled her off of the book and—"

"Wait a minute!" Zack broke in, sitting up alertly, his earlier dream-like mood shattered. "What do you mean, '*pulled her off of the book*'?"

Megan's frown deepened.

"She had her face in it."

"Reading it?"

"No—" and a puzzled tone came into Megan's voice. "Funny, I didn't think about it then. The book was flat on the desk and she was crushing her face against it. It was weird."

Zack stared at her.

"Had she passed out or something?"

"I guess. She might have. She sure came to life when he snatched that book away. Almost dragged her head off the desk. But—" and Megan paused again.

"But?" prompted Zack.

She shrugged.

"It's—it's like she was *stuck* to it. That can't be right," she muttered, more to herself.

"How do you mean?"

She looked at Zack, her eyes suddenly glaring.

"*I* don't know," she retorted, annoyed. "It looked like he had to hold on to her head to pry her loose from the book. But that doesn't make sense—maybe I'm not remembering it the way it happened. It all happened so fast..." and her voice faded to silence again.

She looked upset at the memory.

"Was that all?" asked Zack, less intensely. He had noted her expression.

"No," she said slowly, "There was something else. A smell. A *nasty* smell. It about made me puke my guts out right there on the counter."

Zack thought this information over and snorted derisively.

"Probably farted," he drawled contemptuously.

Megan laughed at this juvenile riposte but shook her head.

"I thought of that too—but it wasn't that kind of smell. It was—ugly. Like something died."

She shuddered and turned pale.

"I don't want to talk about it," she said in a whisper and suddenly leaned forward, clutching her arms tightly to her sides.

Zack stared at her for a moment, then swiftly moved closer to her, putting his arm on her shoulder.

"Baby?" he asked, his voice anxious and concerned, "Are you all right? What's wrong?"

Megan stiffened and partially raised herself up, still clutching her arms around her middle. Her eyes were wide as she turned her face towards Zack's.

"What—*what did you just call me?*" she asked, hardly daring to breathe.

Zack's face flushed but he did not take his arm from her shoulder.

"*'Baby,'*" he repeated, softly. "You don't mind if I call you that? You didn't before—" and he fell silent.

She slowly drew herself back to a sitting position, staring at him speechlessly. The two of them locked eyes for a moment, the silence roaring in their ears.

Megan suddenly started to cry. She didn't attempt to fight it; she didn't even try to hide it. The tears welled up; she trembled and started sobbing as though her heart would break. She leaned back against his arm and suddenly he was holding her, drawing her to him; she wrapped her arms around him and held him tightly, crying into his neck.

Zack gently massaged her shoulder and stroked her hair. Her hot tears stung his skin. He held her closely, remaining silent.

Her shaking finally subsided and she righted herself, pulling herself out of his embrace. Fumbling in her purse, she fished out some tissues, wiped her eyes and blew her nose. Disheveled and vulnerable, she dropped all pretense of indifference and said to him in an accusing voice, "Why did you ask me to dinner tonight?"

He looked at her with a bleak, desolate expression of utter despair. She waited for his reply, frightened at the intensity of his look.

"Because I missed you," he said, simply.

Disbelief flooded her face.

"You *missed* me?" she repeated.

He shrugged.

"That was part of it," he replied and turned his face away from her.

She waited, her heart pounding.

"What else, then?" she finally asked.

He let out a deep sigh.

"Balance," he said, quietly.

She regarded him mutely, her eyes flashing.

"Balance?" she repeated softly. Her voice had an alarming edge, but he did not react to it.

"Yeah," he replied, leaning back against the couch and closing his eyes. All of his alertness had vanished into a gloomy demeanor of surrender: like a man hearing the door lock from inside the execution chamber.

"I had a very interesting conversation with Mark about that, this afternoon," he continued, his voice flat and toneless.

"About *balance?*" she queried, at a loss for the moment.

Zack nodded.

"Sort of," he said, choosing his words carefully. Megan noted the tension in his face, the defeat in his voice, his clenched hands, tight jaw and suddenly realized what a risk it was for him to share these feelings with her. Her annoyance faded away and she listened intently, trying hard to let him speak without prompting.

"We were talking about the same stuff I've always tried to talk to you about. He—he *knows* what's going on more than anyone else I've met before."

Megan, frightened at the unexpected direction the conversation was taking, hung on anxiously to every word.

"It wasn't until I thought about it afterward that I realized we really were talking about something else" and he shook his head slightly as if still amazed at his discovery.

She looked at him, fearfully.

"I'm afraid I've been lying to you, Baby," he said finally and opened his eyes, staring straight into hers with the same chilling glance as before.

She wanted to say something but her throat was too tight for her voice to work.

He looked up at the ceiling.

"I've been going on for years about how no one understands anything that I say, that nobody gets my point of view, no one cares, frustrated for years," he continued, almost as though talking to himself.

Then he looked right at her and she shuddered.

"It never occurred to me that *I* didn't *'get it'* either."

Her fear vanished and she felt—uncertain. She had no idea what to do or say. This was unfamiliar territory and she was lost in its darkness.

"I wasted all those years being angry for nothing—" and he stopped, hanging his head.

He shook and wiped his forearm across his eyes.

Megan took a deep breath, then reached out her arms toward him. The instant her fingers touched him he turned around and suddenly they were in each other's arms, their mouths locked, their bodies writhing in a flaming, passionate embrace. He pulled her down, she followed and they continued the endless dance—lost in the sounds of their music.

Finally, they broke loose and just lay next to each other, their hands linked together and breathing in unison.

The clock read midnight.

"Babe?" asked Megan.

"Yeah," replied Zack.

"I have to get home."

Neither of them moved.

"Do you really want to go?" he asked.

She didn't blush.

"No," she admitted.

He squeezed her hand tighter.

"You can use my room," he said, carefully rising to a sitting position. "I can sleep out here," and he stood up, a little unsteady on his feet. He reached down, assisted Megan to rise and they both walked toward Zack's bedroom, arms around their waists.

"Oh—" gasped Megan as she caught sight of a glass cat sitting on a shelf.

Zack hung his head and said nothing.

Tears formed in her eyes.

"Why—why did you keep it? How *could* you keep it after what—?"

He smiled wearily, his eyes wet.

"I didn't want to lose the memories that went with it," he replied.

Shaking, Megan stared at him, the tears starting to drip down her face. Zack reached out and gently dried one off her cheek with his fingers. She suddenly reached out, pressed his hand against her face, and kissed it, tenderly.

"Oh Megan—" breathed Zack but he was no longer able to say anything.

The clock read two-thirty.

Inside and outside it was deathly quiet. Megan woke up with a start, frantically gazing around in the darkness for the source of the sound that had shocked her into consciousness.

The choking sound.

"Zack?"

She gently touched the sleeping form next to her.

There was no response.

"Zack? Baby? What's wrong?"

Terror swept over her as Zack began moaning and writhing into the pillow, gasping and struggling with flailing arms. The sweat poured down his enfevered face. He cried out again and collapsed—his body cold and still.

"Zack—for gawd's sake—*wake up!*" she cried out, shaking him.

A convulsion rippled through him and the cries and writhing began again. His moaning became more intense and his body spasmed as though electrocuted. He collapsed again, insensible.

Megan, her face haggard, shook him violently by the shoulders but there was still no response. Panic seized her completely and she slapped him hard across the face, first to the left and then to the right, screaming out, "Zack!" in an anguished voice.

His eyes flew open on the second contact and he froze, staring at her as though he did not recognize her. Then he suddenly began scrambling, trying to get free of the blankets and her grip with a naked expression of fear in his eyes. Megan lunged forward, wrapped herself tightly around him, pressing into him, pulling him back down onto the bed, feeling his struggles surge as he redoubled his efforts to break loose. She hung on to him grimly.

Then the terror in his eyes changed to recognition followed by relief. He wrapped himself around her, trembling almost as much as she was, and collapsed into her arms.

"Baby, Baby," she kept repeating softly, stroking his back and hair, "It's okay. It's okay."

His trembling ceased and he relaxed, submitting to her embrace. She gently moved him so she could see his face and then hugged him tightly again, tears in her eyes as she spoke, "My gawd Baby! What happened to you? What's wrong?"

Zack sighed and held her tightly as she curled around him.

"Oh my gawd," he moaned and trembled again.

"Baby—what happened? I was so scared! *You wouldn't wake up!*" At this memory, her tears increased. "I thought I had lost you," she said with a catch in her voice. "Were you having a bad dream?"

He rambled disjointedly, his voice muffled in the closeness of their embrace. Megan's anxiety had painfully sharpened her hearing but she could only catch a few indistinct words. Only one of them came through clearly—

"*Strangled?*" she repeated, alarmed. "Is *that* what you just said?"

Zack loosened her arms and reached for his throat—rubbing it and wincing as though it pained him. He took several gasping deep breaths. Then he held her closely and put his hands on each side of her face. She grabbed them and pressed them closer, staring at him anxiously.

His face was gentle.

"I love you, Megan," he said.

She buried her face in his shoulder.

"I love you too," she whispered.

They clung together for a long time, gradually calming. At last, their breathing became deeper and the tension vanished from their muscles. Megan gently laid him back down and snuggled next to him, tenderly stroking his cheek.

Zack was silent for a while.

"Baby?" he asked.

She nodded.

"You remember this afternoon, when we were talking about the hidden pictures? How I said I never could '*get them?*'"

She nodded again, concern flooding her face.

He closed his eyes.

"I think I just did. *And I hope to God I never do again.*"

5

STRANGULATORUM

The clock read ten.

The office was silent, its dark windows staring emptily at the parking lot.

The cleaning crew arrived, deactivated the perimeter alarm and set about their tasks of wiping, dumping and dusting. Brooms swept, vacuums roared, the dumpster lid slammed as they bagged and purged the last remains of the day. Dispensers were refilled, disinfectant sprayed, fixtures were scrubbed, polished and rinsed.

At last, the mop was wrung dry and the bucket rinsed out. Doors were closed, lights turned off and the perimeter alarm reactivated. From the parking lot came a brief cacophony of car doors slamming, heated conversations, ignitions firing and engines starting that quickly faded into silence as the cleaning crew continued their nightly quest to its next destination.

Only the perpetual hum of the streetlights and the distant, monotonous roar of the freeway remained to break the silence of the night.

There was no wind. The temperature dropped below freezing.

The clock read eleven-thirty.

A mysterious figure, keeping to the shadows, stealthily made its way from the adjacent parking lot toward the back door of the office. The surveillance cameras displayed a slim person wrapped tightly in a full-length coat with a hood pulled completely over its face. It reached the back door, stopped, fished in its pockets and pulled out a key. A moment later the back door opened and the figure slipped inside, quietly shutting the door behind it. A few seconds later, the system log recorded the deactivation of the perimeter alarm using the supervisor's code.

Donna, breathing harshly like a marathon runner fresh from a race, pushed her hood back and stood by the alarm panel. She held out a hand against the wall to steady herself and kept looking around her in the darkness as though afraid of being seen.

A closer glance would have revealed that fear was not the only factor involved: the red flush of guilt suffused her face.

She became aware of this feeling and angrily shook it off.

Leaving the lights off, she crept down the hallway into the break room. She let out an irritated gasp as she saw the padlock hanging from Mark's locker. For a moment, she stood with her fists clenched at her sides, stymied. Then she walked determinedly over to the supply room door, unlocked it and started fossicking around the shelves in the dark. She found the tool she wanted, carefully removed it from the shelf and walked back into the break room. She went directly to Mark's locker and sliced through the hasp with a grim looking pair of bolt cutters, wincing as the mutilated fragments clanged on the floor.

Leaving the bolt cutters on the table, she carefully lifted out the remnants of the hasp and tossed them on the floor. The door squeaked outrageously as she opened the locker, reached inside with trembling hands, fumbled for a moment, and retrieved the book, an expression of triumph polluting her features with a sinister glow. She carefully shut the door and stood for a moment, clutching it to her chest like a wildcat with its prey.

Then she turned and walked down the hall, her footsteps echoing slightly in the stillness. She threaded her way through the spectral shadows of the counter area, illuminated by the faint glow of the computer screens and furiously blinking status lights. Reaching her office at last, she passed through the open door, sat down at her desk and placed the book in front of her.

She shivered. Dizziness suddenly swept through her and she sunk her face into her hands, her memory unwillingly recalling that strange experience of the afternoon—the bizarre fantasy that ended abruptly when Mark pushed her face away, slamming her against the back of her chair—

Pushed her face away.

The dizziness vanished and she frowned, her eyes still closed.

That didn't make sense—how could he have gotten close enough to push her face away without her seeing him approach? She tried to recall the details that led up to that moment but her memory stubbornly refused to cooperate. She was sitting in her chair. Mark was standing up. What had she been doing before he touched her? How had he gotten that close to her? And why did her memory replay the scene with him *'pushing her away?' Away from what?*

She strove to break free from this train of thought but struggling only seemed to make her memories more vivid. Something else must have happened too—*what could it have been?*

Pain. That was part of it. Pain. A crushing, debilitating pain. But where had she felt it? In her chest? No. Her head? Close. Her neck? She shivered again and suddenly raised her head upright, her hands gingerly fondling her neck with hypersensitive fingers.

It was still sore. She winced as she circled around her throat. The front and back of her neck were tender to the touch.

She shook her head slightly.

That couldn't be right—

She glared disdainfully at the book lying before her as though it were Mark himself. Her lips curled and she made a contemptuous spitting sound. *That arrogant weed!* Where does *he* get off with his cocky self-assurance? How dare he try to control me? Does he really think he can play the game as well as I can? Yes, he's won the first few rounds but that was just feinting on my part. I *let* him win those. Once he's fooled into feeling secure I'll turn on him when he least expects it and rip his ego to shreds, crushing the whimpering fragments cruelly under my heels—

The twisted grimace froze on her face as she sucked in her breath sharply.

The book was glowing from inside the cover.

She jumped up quickly and backed cautiously away from the desk, groping along the wall, fighting a growing urge to look behind her, her fury now transformed into an ice-cold shroud of terror. The blood-red glow from the pages deepened. Unable to tear her eyes away from the sight, she continued backwards along the wall, her panic growing worse with each step. Her nostrils flared as she caught the scent of smoke—the glow suddenly obscured by dark plumes rising from the desk as though the book was burning its way through the surface.

She gave a sharp croak from her tight throat as she noticed a change in the glowing object. What was that strange shape in the middle—no, the *two* strange shapes? Were those eyes? *Eyes that stared at her unblinkingly with inhuman cruelty and hunger?* And those things suddenly crawling from beneath the covers—arms? *Tentacles?*

Her fingers suddenly encountered the hard bulge of the light switch and she desperately snapped it on. There was a blinding flash and she fell to the ground with a cry of pain as though stabbed through the eyes, the dagger ripping down to her midriff as she writhed on the carpet in agony. A strange, choking roar sounded—

And all was quiet as before.

She was lying prone on the floor of her office in dead silence.

Shaken and frightened, she staggered to her feet and unwillingly looked back at the desk. Her eyes nearly burst from her head.

The book lay on the desk as she had placed it there when she first brought it in. No glow. No smoke.

No tentacles. *No eyes.*

Trembling, she forced herself up from the floor, stood up unsteadily and shuffled back to her chair, collapsing in it as though her knees had failed her. She unconsciously ran her fingers through her hair, cringed and gasped with disgust, pulling her fingers free, staring at them with wide eyes.

Her fingers were glistening with sweat. Her hair and scalp were drenched with it. A faint film of it was on her face and all over her skin. She quickly looked back at the book; it still lay on the desk as she'd originally placed it. There were no signs of burning or scorching; the glossy white cover sullenly reflected the lights above it, immutable and unchangeable as always.

She leaned her elbows on the table and pressed her fingers to her temples, trying desperately to hold on to her thoughts. There was something else she was trying to remember— something she felt was vitally important to recall at that exact moment. But her rambling thoughts remained perversely beyond her control.

Pushing her away? No! *That wasn't it at all.*

Mark was pushing something *off* her. Something she could not remember. Her mind clouded as the dizziness overcame her again—but out of the enveloping fog she had this strange vision of Mark with a whip in his hand, loathing on his face, ferociously beating something back like a lion-tamer trying to regain control over a rogue—

She shook herself furiously and her vision cleared. She was sitting in her office, at her desk, the lights glaring painfully in her eyes. Her anger surged, pulsing loudly in her blood, her fingers hooked like the talons of an eagle, her nails sharp as steel. *I could slash his face to ribbons.*

A clear vision of Mark again appeared in her mind and she let out a roar of rage and defiance, slamming her hands painfully on the unyielding desk surface.

'Do not read this book alone. It's dangerous.'

She gritted her teeth at the memory of his voice but turned it into a hissing sneer. Dangerous. *Right.* She drew herself up. She *was* alone—nothing had happened to *her.*

But the vision of Mark persisted, his voice tormenting her as he continued, *'Reading it in your office with the door closed is suicidal.'*

She shuddered and let out a scream of rage.

I'll go the son of a bitch one better! She leaped to her feet, deliberately walked over to her door, seized the knob and slammed the door shut, punching the lock button, the shade slats rattling. An unexpectedly loud hollow boom shook the floor with a reverberating echo that died away reluctantly. The noise frightened her and she paused, paralyzed, until the last echo faded to silence. Then, revolted with her timidity, she shot her middle finger at the door as though Mark were there to see, sticking her tongue out tauntingly as if again screaming out defiance of his power. She walked back to her chair and flung herself in it, breathing hard with moans that were barely human.

I want that picture. I've got to find that picture. I know I saw it—it's in there somewhere. I need to find it so I can smash it in his snot-nosed arrogant face—! Even as she repeated this echoing litany in her head, her memories were troubling her and a chill came over the heat of her anger.

Those pages weren't blank. She *had* seen something on them—she was sure it was pornographic. It certainly affected her that way—that strange mixture of disgust and desire that never failed to arouse her perverse senses. She wouldn't have reacted that way if it *wasn't* pornographic—*but why could she not remember what it looked like?*

Her mind kept recalling strange glistening green and bronze curves, winding cords, spirals...but beyond that point the vision metamorphosed into something else—something that filled her with an unreasoning terror. Something she could not survive the sight of. She remembered feeling her skin prickling, her hair rising, her muscles tensing, her lungs desperately sucking in air—frantic struggles to break free—and finally, everything swallowed up in darkness. The whole process repeated itself over and over like an endless loop in her head. She began shaking as she felt the dizziness creeping into her brain again.

Cowering, she coiled in her chair, both hands shielding the back of her head, her arms tight against her ears as though bracing herself for a sound or blow beyond her strength to bear. Winding herself tighter and tighter, squirming—

She suddenly sat bolt upright, paralyzed with fright, her mind ripped free of the spell and blindingly clear, her muscles painfully taut. Leaping to her feet she looked frantically around the office in terror like an animal cornered by a deadly pursuer.

But there were no hiding places. There was no one, nothing to see. Despite this evidence, her panic fit did not abate in the least—she remained writhing in its grip, hyperventilating, convinced that someone, or something, had her under observation.

Hostile observation.

But there still was nothing to see.

With a great mental effort, she forced herself to ignore her fear and slammed herself back down in her chair with a snarl, leaning back and crossing her arms over her chest. Her eyes glinted with fierce determination but she still trembled and kept glancing over her shoulder—as though she couldn't quite shake free of her uneasiness.

She stared grimly at the book lying on her desk. It still appeared to be nothing more than a plain, white ledger with a blank dust jacket. And yet there was something fascinating about it, something mysterious and alluring in its very simplicity that ensnared her senses.

Entranced, she slowly reached out, touched the cover and gave a little shriek of pain, pulling her hand back and sticking her throbbing fingertips in her mouth. Glaring at the book, outraged as though a favorite pet had bitten her, she gingerly pulled her fingers from her mouth and stared at them: *they were blistered and blackened as though they had been burned.*

Her hands shook.

She forced them down against the desk, leaning on them, but the shaking merely transferred to her arms. She could not stop the tremors. She struggled uselessly for a few minutes trying to bring herself back under control but her will to resist suddenly failed, forcing her to abandon her efforts.

Fighting an unexpected reluctance, she cautiously reached out for the book again, suddenly tearing the cover open with a savage gesture, ignoring the pain shooting through her fingers, past her wrist, into her arm. She reached out again and stopped, horrified at the bright red stains on the clean white paper, dripping on the desk surface. Her nerves screamed as she realized the stains were coming from her fingertips, a slow, steady, oozing drip as though her fingers had been scored with a razor blade. She stared at the stains mutely. Her eyes widened as she heard hissing and saw faint puffs of smoke rise every time a drop of blood hit the page. *Like ice water dripping on a hot iron...*

Then her anger returned and she stared straight at the book again, right into the page.

Except for the bloodstains, the page was blank without a mark on it.

She turned the page.

Still blank.

She turned another page and went cold: the eyes she had seen earlier were staring at her, their inhuman cold-blooded glare clutching at her heart as the feeling she was being watched suddenly returned. She struggled to push her chair back from the desk but she could not move the chair an inch. She felt her chest pressing into the edge and realized the chair was being pushed from behind. She was trapped.

Her vision rapidly dimming, she blindly reached out, groped for the edge of the page and turned it over with all of her strength.

The panic vanished, her vision cleared and she felt the chair give back a little. The pressure left her chest and she gasped, breathing shallowly, her heart racing, by now her whole body shaking uncontrollably. Her lip trembled.

She glanced at the locked door longingly, tears welling up in her eyes, but it was too far away for her to reach. Even if she had the strength to stand up she would have collapsed immediately. Crawling to the door would be useless; she would never have been able to raise herself off the floor to reach the knob; no one would be able to hear her cries in time to save her. For a moment she sat limply in her chair, beaten, defeated.

After a few minutes, she sat up, glancing hopelessly at the door once more. Still consumed with her quest for the elusive picture, she forced her arm, with all of her remaining strength, back out to the book and turned yet another page, staring at it fearfully.

It was blank.

She turned another page and suddenly the pain in her arm inflamed, flowing to her neck. She clamped her jaws together so tightly her teeth were jammed into the gums. She whimpered. The room started to swim.

Tears poured from her eyes as she shook her head, her lips quavering as her faint cries of, "No, no," degenerated to wordless sounds squeezed out of lungs unable to draw breath. Powerless, as though detached from her body, she watched her hand reach out again and again, forced to turn page after page, each effort more painful than the one before, writhing in a growing ecstasy of torture until her strength deserted her arms completely. She slumped to her forearms, no longer able to support her upper body, hunched down with her face only inches from the paper. It wasn't until the first wave of retching took her that she became aware of the smell.

No—the *stench*. An eye-burning reek, a nauseous perfume exuding from the page that clutched her stomach and twisted her agonized intestines with steely claws. She retched again and struggled to raise her head.

She could not do it.

It was as though something were holding her down.

Or was something *pulling* her down?

She struggled to rise again and her forearms slipped, her face crashing into the smoking paper. A burning sensation instantly engulfed her head as she flailed her now useless arms, her inarticulate cries smothered in the paper, desperately trying to pull herself free of the poisonous fumes devouring her reason. The heat suddenly intensified, her whole being paralyzed with terror as she realized what was happening: *she was being pulled out of her chair onto the desk.*

Vainly twisting and turning, the inexorable force steadily dragged her up from her seat, her useless legs dangling limply behind her. She felt a shock of pain as her knees slammed against the edge of the desk; her shins rubbed raw as they scraped across the sharp corner. The pain flared and flamed up and down her spine. Her knees burned as they skidded across the hot metal surface.

Her head suddenly plunged abruptly downward as though she were flinging herself over the edge of a steep cliff. She instinctively pushed back with her hands as she felt herself continuing over but her palms encountered nothing but empty space. Her hair pulled at her head; it burst into flames with a crackling noise. She started slipping rapidly and the scream began forming itself from the bottom of her throat, gathering force as her neck constricted, preparing to launch itself from her mouth in an explosion of anguish, terror and pain—the intensity tearing her vocal chords raw and bloody, spitting out the foul remnants—

6

RECOIL

Oatmeal.
Oatmeal and bacon.
Oatmeal, bacon, coffee, toast—
Zack wearily opened his eyes as the scents grew stronger. Still in the grips of dream-paralysis, he wondered at first why he was having delusions of food. As his senses slowly came to full attention, he felt a glow of peaceful happiness seeping through his pores and closed his eyes, savoring the pleasurable sensations, long forgotten, sweeping through him. The sudden clatter of dishes from the kitchen did nothing to dispel them.

He slowly pushed back the sheets and blankets and sat up in the bed, stretching. Almost afraid to look, he quickly glanced at the opposite side of the mattress and was rewarded with the sight of the extra pillows snuggled next to his, freed from their accustomed resting place in the storage closet, their dinted surfaces testifying to recent use.

Rising to his feet with a yawn, he shivered as the cool air of the apartment struck his naked skin. Hugging himself, he padded over to the closet, slid the door open and fished out an ankle length black robe, knotting it tightly. His slippers were sitting at their usual spot next to the door. He slid his feet into their warmth and made his way to the kitchen, smiling at the unaccustomed sound of activity within.

"Good morning, love," he said as he entered.

The figure dressed in his sweats standing by the sink whirled to face him, coffee cup in hand. Megan, her face flushed and her blue eyes shot with pain, looked at him tensely, waiting for him to speak.

Zack smiled even wider. The sight of her in his kitchen was more spectacularly beautiful than a vision of the sweetest of angels. She recognized that feeling in his eyes, carefully set the cup down and walked toward him.

"Good morning," she whispered as they wrapped their arms around each other and kissed deeply.

They pulled their faces apart for a moment, both of them gently caressing each other's back, gazing at each other with pure, undiluted love.

"What?" she finally asked as he continued to gaze at her, dreamily.

"I was hoping it wasn't a dream—I really wanted to find you here," he said.

She quickly turned her face away and continued to cling to him. He squeezed harder and released her. She walked back to the stove to retrieve her cup.

"How did you know what I liked for breakfast?" he asked.

"I pay attention to *some* details," she replied.

He looked over at the kitchen table and was surprised to see it set with plates, utensils and food at the ready.

"How long have you been up?" he asked, looking at the clock. It read six.

"Since about five," she replied, busying herself with the teapot.

He stood uncertainly at the table.

"Aren't you going to eat?" she asked, turning around and bringing a steaming cup to the table.

The uncertainty left him.

"Only if you sit with me," he responded.

She laid his cup down and walked to the opposite end of the table where her plates were waiting.

"No, Baby," he said, firmly. She looked up at him with surprise.

He deliberately walked over to her place setting and moved it so she was sitting right at the corner next to him. She momentarily hid her face again, then smiled, glowing joyfully and sat in the chair he pulled out for her.

They looked at each other, gripped hands and then started eating breakfast. At one point she rose and refilled his cup for him. A few minutes later he did the same for her, with a smile. Finally, they leaned back in their chairs and emitted sighs of satisfaction.

She giggled. He glanced at her with a smile.

The clock read six-twenty.

Noticing the time, he rose from the table. She followed suit.

"I gotta get set to go," he said, but to her surprise he made no move to leave the kitchen. Instead, he started gathering up the plates and utensils, carrying them to the sink.

"Wait a minute!" she cried out, dismayed. He turned to her.

"*You* did the dishes last night. It's only fair—" she protested, but he approached her and gently laid his finger on her lips. She kissed it.

"You can put the stuff away," he said.

She gathered up the cream and orange juice containers while he busied himself at the sink. Finishing first, she made her way out of the kitchen into the living room while he put the final touches on the dishes. After wiping off the table and counter, he wrung out the cloth and hung it across the tap. Then he walked out to the living room after her.

She was standing in front of the main window staring into the fog. The sun was still behind the mountains and the darkness as deep as ever. He stood next to her, the sweet softness of her hip melting into his. Putting his arm around her waist was as natural a thing as her leaning into him as they both stared into the fog together.

"Megan," he began and she looked at him. She was still a little nervous and a faint sheen of worry clouded her eyes, but the happiness she felt was too strong to dissipate at this point.

"Yes?" she replied softly, caressing his hip where she'd placed her hand.

He cleared his throat, still staring out into the fog.

"Would it be easier for you to move in with me or the other way around?"

"Oh!" She sucked in her breath and they both turned and faced each other.

She stared at him.

"I mean it, Baby," he said.

She made no effort to hide the water in her eyes; it slowly overflowed and seeped down her face.

"Are you sure you want to do this?" she asked, so softly he could hardly hear her.

He pulled her closer.

"Maybe we should just pick out a new place instead?" he asked.

He pulled her to him as he saw her nodding her head, absently reaching out her hand to wipe the moisture off her face. He bent down, kissed her hand, licked the tears off it tenderly and they embraced again, their mutual heat flaming between them.

They finally separated but still held on to each other tightly. She buried her face in his chest.

"I don't want to let you go," he said, stroking her hair, "I'm afraid if I do you'll vanish."

"That's why I don't want to let *you* go," she said, her voice muffled by his chest.

Zack stretched without releasing her and looked down at her as she raised her head, gazing at him nakedly.

He continued to stroke her hair and face for a while, then looked at the clock and sighed.

"You taken a shower yet?" he asked.

She shook her head as she looked at the clock herself.

"Care to join me?"

She looked up at him sharply. His eyes twinkled.

Arms linked, they made their way to the bathroom together.

It was a beautiful morning.

The sun pushed its way over the mountains, its pale light flooding across an unusual cloudless winter sky. The fog was rapidly melting away with little phantom patches remaining behind here and there. The spider webs shimmered like tinsel in the evergreens and flickers of light winked where the sun's rays struck patches of ground water.

Megan sighed and leaned over in her seat, clutching Zack's arm as they drove through the icy streets to the office. She raised herself up and kissed his cheek. He smiled but did not take his eyes off the road. The ice glittered wickedly on the pavement; he was taking no chances.

They swung into the empty parking lot.

"Looks like we're the first ones here," he said.

She snuggled closer.

He slid into a parking space and shut off the engine, releasing his seat belt at the same time. He turned toward her. The sight of her face, still glowing with love and desire was too strong to resist and they found themselves kissing again.

The sound of an approaching engine caused them to spring apart guiltily; Zack straightened his uniform shirt and Megan gently touched up her hair. Both of them looked at each other, saw their mutual blush and giggled as they opened the doors.

They stepped out into the clear, cold air, their breath smoking from their mouths, shut the doors and walked carefully across the frosted parking lot.

They had to fight hard to not link arms.

The car they had heard swung into view. It was Mark, his immaculate machine shining in the sunlight. He waved at them as he parked; they waited for him in the middle of the lot.

"You guys are early today," he said by way of greeting.

"Guess it's the trend today," replied Zack.

Mark shut and locked his door, then narrowed his eyes and scanned the parking lot.

As he walked toward them, he said to Megan:

"Where is your car? Did you walk here?"

Before Megan could answer, Zack replied, "She rode in with me."

Mark stopped and looked dead straight into Zack's unwavering eye. A slow smile crossed his face and he raised his eyebrow briefly.

"Thank you," said Zack.

Megan looked blankly at both of them but Mark nodded his head, smiled warmly and continued walking toward them.

"I forgot my purse!" exclaimed Megan suddenly, turning to Zack in a fright.

Zack gently patted her shoulder and handed her his keys. Megan quickly walked across the lot to the car.

Zack followed her with his eyes, then turned back to Mark. His smile faded as Mark approached, disturbed by some subtle change in his demeanor: his usually impassive face was marred with a tinge of uncertainty. Zack was even more surprised to notice that his eyes were constantly darting to his left and right as though anticipating trouble of some kind.

"Mark? Are you okay?" asked Zack, surprised at his boldness.

Mark took the inquiry in stride however and just shook his head wearily. *Wearily?*

"I guess so," he said with a sigh. This only increased Zack's worry.

"What's wrong, then?"

"I don't know," said Mark slowly, "I'm picking up really strange vibes for some reason—no!" he suddenly emphasized as Zack's face clouded slightly, "nothing to do with *that*."

Mark stopped in front of Zack and suddenly stared straight at him as though amazed. His eyes widened and he slowly reached out his hand toward Zack's throat. Zack stepped back in alarm.

"What are you doing—?" began Zack but Mark caught himself at this and forced his hand down to his side. His face was livid.

"Did you have—bad dreams last night?" asked Mark, as though hardly daring to breathe.

Zack's memory of that nightmare had vanished in the morning light. Now it returned, as intense as it was when Megan slapped him awake. As the recollection of its horror spread across his suddenly pale face, he was dismayed to see Mark's face harden, his hands curling into fists.

"What is it?" asked Zack in a tone nearly equal to Mark's.

Mark looked at the office—Zack's terror increasing at the expression on his face.

"We've got to get in there," Mark muttered.

They both walked quickly toward the back door. Zack reached for his keys, then remembered Megan still had them. He turned to call her but she ran up as he did this and put the keys into his outstretched hand.

"Zack—what?" she cried in surprise as both he and Mark broke into a run toward the back door. She followed instinctively at the same pace.

Mark tried the door but it was locked. Zack quickly keyed it open and they passed inside together. Mark had his hand on the light switch when they all froze at the sound of Zack's voice.

"Wait a minute!" he barked.

They looked at him, wonderingly.

"The alarm. *The alarm isn't going off.*"

Mark was puzzled.

"What about it?"

He looked at Megan and was surprised to see her just as upset as Zack.

"The last person out is supposed to set the alarm," she explained in a shocked voice.

Mark did not see why this was so important.

"Someone else must have got here before us then," he shrugged.

"Then where is their car?" asked Zack.

Mark, impatient to keep going, responded distractedly, "Maybe the cleaning crew forgot to set it or something?"

Zack shook his head reluctantly as Mark continued down the hall. The other two followed, Megan muttering, "It would be the first time in fifteen years they did."

Mark's strange mood began to affect Megan and Zack. They found themselves scanning behind them frequently, although they had no idea what they were looking for. Mark, still in front, merely gave the break room a quick glance from the doorway as he passed it. Megan and Zack were following him when Megan suddenly gasped and cried out, "Zack!" pointing with one hand into the break room and clutching his arm with the other.

Zack looked over at her sharply as she forced him to halt.

"What is it?" he asked, alert.

She pointed wordlessly at the remains of the padlock scattered on the floor.

"What the hell?" he breathed. He gently released himself from Megan, walked in rapidly and leaned toward the floor for a closer look, freezing as felt a hand on his shoulder.

"What are you looking at?" asked Mark, even as he saw the bolt cutters on the table and the mutilated lock lying on the floor. His face instantly went black with anger and he rushed over to his locker, opened the door, reached inside for a moment, stiffened, then dashed toward the counter area. Zack and Megan looked at each other in amazement and quickly followed him.

Mark ran through the counter area and stopped at the door to Donna's office with a cry of rage and despair. Zack and Megan, right behind, nearly knocked each other over trying to avoid running into him. They clung together, watching Mark with wide eyes.

"My gawd," whispered Zack, nudging Megan, "the lights—"

Megan looked and gave a stifled exclamation.

The hallway, the break room and the counter area were in darkness as was the lobby. But the door and window into Donna's office were outlined by a powerful white glare from inside the room. The window shade did nothing to abate it. The brightness was almost too intense to be real; an unbearable luminescence that burned their eyes painfully as though the sun itself was behind the door.

Mark bent forward, shielding his eyes, trying to pick out a view of the interior through the slats of the shade.

"No!" he muttered to himself, "she couldn't have been that—"

He put his hand on the doorknob and recoiled with a furious cry, shaking his hand as though he had been stung.

At this Megan and Zack, who had frozen in place where they were, broke their stance and rushed forward but they halted again as Mark turned around, his eyes blazing, his hand outstretched in an imperious gesture.

"Stay back!" he snapped sharply. There was no need for further words: the expression on his face was enough to ensure their compliance. Fright seized them as they realized that Mark, Mark the impassable, imperturbable stoic, was *afraid.*

Mark pulled a pair of thick leather gloves out of his coat, slipped them on and gingerly tried the knob again. It did not move. Megan choked at the sizzling sound and the faint trace of smoke rising up from his fingertips; *it was as though they had been scorched.* As the whiff of the burning reached Zack he suddenly turned pale and swayed where he stood, in the grip of a vivid memory he did not want to recall.

Mark hesitated, stepped back and then, with an inarticulate shout, twisted his body into a pivot kick straight at the door.

The lock tore free of the molding and the door flew open, slamming against the wall so hard that all the hanging pictures in the office slid to the floor together in a single unified crash of shattering glass.

Zack and Megan immediately jumped back as a foul reek poured out of the office—doubly horrifying because it was familiar to them. Megan caught a glimpse of the office interior, gave a strangled cry and ran frantically out of the counter area toward the bathroom, one hand to her mouth, the other clutching her stomach. Zack, his eyes squinting against the glare, took one look and rushed over to the counter phone, frantically punching 911. As the stench drifted out of the office and engulfed him he leaned forward with eyes clenched shut and an arm around his stomach, struggling desperately against the urge to vomit his heart out.

Unaffected by the polluted air, Mark stood in the doorway, regarding the scene coldly. He could see Donna, lying as he had found her that afternoon, her face mashed into the open pages of the book. A pool of blood dripped from beneath her face, soaking the pages, overflowing onto the desk surface and congealing into a thick sticky mass with rivulets running off the edge. Her head was barely visible amidst the cruel light blasting from the pages.

Mark stared at her for a moment, livid. Then he strode through the doorway over to the desk, grabbed the back of her neck, placed his other hand firmly on the book and threw her back into her chair hard enough to shatter her skull. He gave a grunt of disgust as he stared grimly at the wreckage left behind. The surface of the book was awash in blood mixed with fragments of flesh and bone.

Her face had been ripped off her skull, her eye sockets empty and bleeding, her teeth exposed in a perpetual grimace of horror, her throat crushed and neck twisted. Mark glared at her contemptuously.

"You asked for it," he muttered.

He carefully pried the book loose from her fingers. Zack looked inside from the counter as he passed on information to the first responders, his eyes riveted on Mark who was stalking aimlessly inside the office, looking up and down and around him, muttering to himself, holding the open book in front of him.

Zack's attention diverted back to the telephone; he turned away from the doorway as he spoke into the receiver. He hung up the phone and nearly jumped out of his skin as a violent report shook the room. His senses raging with fright, he turned back to the office and stared at the now closed door. The window glass was splintered. An unaccountable wave of terror took possession of him and he felt his legs giving way beneath him, his vision blurring dangerously—

"*Open the f— door!*" Mark's voice roared out from within.

Zack caught himself falling and grabbed the back of the chair. The door flew open as though sucked into the office. This time the impact knocked all of the glass out of the window, permanently embedding the knob in the wall, the door hanging precariously from its frame, its hinges bent and torn from their fastenings.

In the meantime, Mark, his face disfigured with loathing and fury, raised up the book slightly and suddenly snapped it shut, clenching the covers tightly in his arms.

Almost as though he was catching something, flashed through Zack's overwrought senses. For a moment, he had the vivid impression that Mark was desperately struggling to prevent the book from forcing itself open. He shook his head, unable to believe his eyes and looked again. This time all he saw was Mark walking out of the office, tears in his eyes and a profound expression of grief on his face, carrying the book under his arm. Zack stared in amazement: *There were no signs of blood or flesh on the clean white paper.* The terrible light from within the pages was gone.

Mark, seeing the look in Zack's eyes, nodded his head, beckoning him to follow.

"Come on," he barked, curtly.

Zack, his strength nearly gone, followed him with tottering steps. Megan, her face still suffused with green, came staggering out of the bathroom as they passed the door, dry heaving as she caught the odor now permeating the building. Zack grabbed her and put his arm protectively around her. Mark turned and looked at them.

"You two," said Mark, flatly, "Get outside and block the door. Don't let anyone in until the police get here. I'll watch the front."

They obeyed without question, walking down the hallway to the door as Mark turned into the break room behind them. They heard the sound of a locker opening and a heart-wrenching sob as they passed through the outside door.

Rolla and Shawn were already there. Kip was just walking up. They all stopped in surprise as Zack and Megan staggered out, shut the door behind them and leaned against it, both of them nearly bent double from fighting their nausea.

"What the hell is going on?" asked Kip wonderingly as Rolla echoed the question. The sirens of the first responders were suddenly audible in the distance, growing closer.

"She's—she's dead," faltered Zack, white and shaking.

"What? Who? Who's dead?" exploded from various throats.

"Donna," said Zack.

Megan suddenly collapsed to her knees and vomited on the sidewalk. Zack immediately knelt at her side.

An ambulance, a fire truck and three police cars whipped into the parking lot with lights and strobes blazing. Doors flew open and people fanned out toward the back door. An unmarked police car roared up and disgorged an older man in a severe blue business suit with cold eyes to match. He walked up to them quickly, flashing a badge at Zack and snapping, "Detective Parnall. What's going on?"

Zack, on his haunches, his hand stroking Megan's back, desperately striving to maintain his cool, looked up, and answered, "There's a dead body inside the building."

Parnall whipped out a notebook and began writing.

"Who discovered the body?"

"The three of us."

"Which three?"

"Me," said Zack, "Megan," he pointed to her crouching figure on the pavement, "and Mark."

"Where's Mark?" asked the detective sharply.

"He's still inside."

The detective's eyes glittered.

"What the hell is he doing in there?"

"Guarding the front door."

The detective frowned as Zack continued, his voice faltering, "He—he saw everything closer than we did."

"What do you mean?"

"He was first in line when we found her."

"Where was that?"

"In her office."

"Who is '*her*'? The body?"

Zack nodded.

"You have any idea who it is?"

"It's our supervisor. Donna Flancher."

The detective thought for a moment.

"Was *he* here first?" he asked, pointing inside the building.

"No, we arrived just before he did."

"You went in together?"

"Yes."

"Notice anything unusual?"

"The alarm wasn't set and the lights were on in her office."

The detective thought for a moment.

"You have surveillance equipment here?"

"Yes," nodded Zack. "There's a system monitoring the parking lot and another inside the building."

The detective nodded as though he had reached a decision.

"Okay. You two leave your names with officer Kalt over there," and he pointed at a young uniformed officer standing a few feet away. "If we need to ask you anything else we'll contact you later."

The detective drew his weapon, clicked off the safety and headed for the door, motioning to two other officers who drew their weapons likewise and joined him. Parnall tried the knob, then turned to Zack.

"Unlock it!" he barked.

Zack gave Megan's shoulder a reassuring squeeze and quickly rose to his feet, keyed open the lock and pulled the door open for them. They rushed inside, weapons at the ready.

"Everyone else stay put!" shouted officer Kalt who maneuvered himself to block the doorway. Zack slowly walked back to Megan and stood next to her, watching her.

Fifteen minutes later another car arrived with the legend **"CORONER"** emblazoned on its doors. A woman accompanied by a man carrying a large hard case got out and walked up to the door.

Kalt, observing their approach, keyed his microphone.

"Okay to let the coroner in?"

"Yeah, we're ready for her. The scene is cleared," came the fuzzy reply.

"You guys are good to go," he said to the team and waved them through into the building.

Kip, Rolla, Shawn and Drak stood aside, muttering to each other and glancing curiously at Zack. Megan staggered to her feet with Zack's assistance and clung to his side, hiding her face in his shoulder. Kip's group, seeing this, stared at them in amazement.

Zack started as an unexpected hand gripped his shoulder.

"You two go home. I'm shutting the office down for the day. None of you are in any shape to be working today."

Lilly's empathetic and grim expression somehow thawed the numbness of the after-shock; a wave of physical and emotional exhaustion washed over them. On impulse, they both reached for Lilly at the same time and all three of them hugged tightly.

Zack, weariness rapidly overcoming him, gave a weak smile and whispered, "Thank you, Lilly."

Lilly pulled them a little closer to her. Then, gently disengaging herself, she gently squeezed their shoulders and again said, "Go home," firmly. She walked away toward the others who were still staring in shocked disbelief.

Lilly showed no overt surprise at Megan and Zack's unexpected display of affection and her face was set hard as she approached the rest of the staff. Only her eyes betrayed the depth of the grief and joy flooding through her.

Zack and Megan watched her for a moment, then turned and looked in each other's face. They were mutually troubled at the intensity of their gazes—each carefully examining the other for a moment. They sighed, joined hands and turned to go.

"Hold on," broke in Kalt and they whirled around. "I need your names."

Zack gave his name and phone number to Kalt. He did not show any reaction when Megan used his phone number for her contact information as well; he simply accepted this as an accomplished fact. Arm in arm, supporting each other, the two of them slowly walked across the parking lot to Zack's car, ignoring their colleagues' incredulous, dumbfounded stares. In contrast, there was a warm smile on Lilly's face. They got inside the car and drove off.

Lilly sighed and turned to face officer Kalt who was watching her warily.

"Yes ma'am?" he asked as she walked up to him.

She pulled out her ID badge and showed it to him.

"I'm the District Manager," she said.

Kalt nodded his head and spoke into his mic again. The radio squawked something unintelligible, but Kalt understood it and nodded to her.

"Go on in, ma'am. Detective Parnall is waiting for you inside."

She pulled opened the door and then stood aside as the first responders made their way through, carrying a stretcher. A shapeless figure wrapped in bloodstained gauze lay strapped to the sheets. Lilly's face turned white but there was no sign of grief in her eyes. The rest of the staff, noticing the absence of an intravenous drip and the ominous sight of an oxygen bottle, bowed their heads and closed their eyes as they carried the stretcher past them to the ambulance. It drove away silently, the flashing lights and strobes turned off.

Again Lilly tried to enter but found her way blocked again, this time by Mark. The expression on his face caught her off guard and she shuddered.

"Mark?" she asked, half-shocked, half-sympathetic, "Are you feeling all right?"

He looked at her, wordlessly, his eyes cold and unreadable. She gasped as she saw the first tears forming but he blinked them back and walked away from her silently, continuing across the parking lot to his car without a word.

"Something wrong, ma'am?" a deep voice behind her inquired. She turned around quickly and saw a cold-eyed man in a business suit watching her closely. Behind her, Mark got into his car, fired up the engine and drove off.

Seeing her discomfort, he continued in a softer voice, "I apologize, ma'am. I didn't mean to startle you. I'm detective Parnall."

A little color came into her face and she instantly regained her poise.

"I'm Lilly Braxton," she said, displaying her ID as they shook hands.

She turned around once more to the parking lot but Mark had already gone. She sighed and turned back to the detective who was still watching her quizzically.

"Is there something wrong?" Parnall asked again.

She shrugged.

"I guess he's really upset about this," she said. "He's usually a lot more confident—" but the detective, his expression neutral again, cut in smoothly and politely motioned to her to precede him down the hallway.

"That's understandable, ma'am," he said as they walked. "It's enough to throw anyone off balance."

The phone rang stridently through the silent apartment. Megan, startled out of a deep sleep, fought her way out of the blankets, fumbled for the phone and answered it with a shaky voice.

"Hello?" she asked.

"Megan?"

Megan could almost see Lilly's eyebrows rise and her smile.

"Yes," she admitted, blushing furiously.

"You okay?"

"I—I—I think so," she stammered.

Lilly's voice went into professional mode.

"Is Zack available?"

"I'll see," she replied and turned to the unconscious figure lying next to her. His breathing was stertorous and he trembled occasionally. Gathering her courage she gently nudged him and his eyes flew open.

He looked at her blankly.

"It's Lilly," said Megan.

Still half-asleep, Zack raised himself up to a sitting position and took the phone from her. Catching her expression, he gently squeezed and kissed her hand. Megan smiled.

"Yeah?" he asked, tersely.

A long conversation followed to which Zack made only non-committal responses, nodding his head or shaking it. At one point his face went completely white and he hung his head. Megan looked at him with mingled love and worry.

"I'm—I'm sorry to hear about that," he said.

Then, "No—no, I'm glad you told me now. It wasn't going to be easy either way."

Megan lay back down and stared at the ceiling, her right hand gently touching his leg.

"Oh? What did they say?"

Zack tensed and sat up a little straighter, a strange unreadable look on his face. Megan sensed the change in his mood and looked at him anxiously.

"You—, are you *sure*, I mean, are *they* sure about that?"

A trace of uneasiness came over Megan as she watched his face; she sat up and moved closer to him.

"They're *that* certain? I mean, there isn't any room for—"

A faint sheen of sweat began gathering on Zack's forehead. Megan put a protective arm around him and gently kissed his cheek. Zack looked at her and gave her a reassuring smile, although it struck her as a bit forced.

"Well, no—I guess I didn't," and Zack swallowed hard, "I mean I didn't go inside and see things up close. I just caught a glimpse and ran to the phone so I suppose I must have missed that," he finally said.

Megan felt him suddenly relax the tension in his muscles; he let out a long sigh.

"No. If that's what they say, I guess that's okay. They know what they're doing."

The conversation continued but Zack did not appear to be listening; he slowly shook his head from side to side as though not convinced. He finally shrugged his shoulders and leaned over to kiss Megan on the forehead. Somewhat reassured, she slowly lay back down next to him. He ran his fingers through her hair.

"Oh—well thank you," he said. "Does that apply to Megan too?"

He blushed.

"Ah yes, no problem. We'll talk about that when we come back. Thank you for calling."

He passed the phone over to Megan and she replaced it in the charger.

They looked at each other for a moment.

Then he reached for her and they embraced, kissing gently.

"I love you, Babe," he said to her.

"I love you too," she replied.

He snuggled next to her and lay on his back as well, staring at the ceiling with her, their hands locked together, fingers gently caressing.

"You know," he said, slowly, "I think I remember you saying something last night about being afraid you'd lost me?"

She pulled his hand to her mouth and kissed it.

"Did you?" he repeated.

Blushing she nodded her head.

He drew her hand to his mouth and kissed it too.

"I don't know what else is going to happen to us," he said, "But I can tell you this much: you are not going to lose me. Never again."

This time their embrace was more passionate, a faint glow of pleasure igniting in their eyes.

They separated for a moment.

Then—

"What did Lilly say?" she asked.

Zack's face became grim and she tensed.

After a long silence, he said, with obvious reluctance, "Lisa died last night in Intensive Care."

Tears came into Megan's eyes and she shook a little.

He looked at her and gently stroked her face.

"Complications or something," he added.

She shook her head and he gently kissed her.

"Oh—" she moaned. He kissed her again and pulled her to him as she began to cry, holding her close and stroking her hair.

"I know, Babe," he said, "It's terrible. I kind of wish I didn't know about it but I'd rather we find out now than when we get back to work."

Megan was still crying softly.

"We have the rest of the week off," he added.

She continued sobbing in his arms.

He held her tightly. She hugged him closer and buried her face in his shoulder, shuddering and snuggling at the same time.

"What else did she tell you?" she asked, finally, raising her head and wiping her eyes.

Zack shook his head.

"She talked to the detective guy this afternoon—I guess they finished the investigation."

Megan looked at him expectantly but he did not seem eager to continue.

"What did they find out?" she prompted.

Zack shrugged.

"They think she killed herself."

Megan's eyes went wide and she turned over on her side, staring at him in amazement.

"How on earth do they figure *that?*" she asked, her tone matching her expression.

Zack remained on his back as he spoke, still staring at the ceiling with a puzzled look on his face.

"Parnall told Lilly they found Donna slumped on the desk, her throat slashed and an open bloodstained straight-razor in her hand. The coroner said that suicide was the only explanation that fit the facts."

"Zack, that's impossible! That *can't* be what happened—" began Megan but Zack shook his head firmly.

"He told Lilly they're *convinced* that's how it happened."

"But she was *killed*—!" protested Megan.

"They don't think so."

"Why?" asked Megan.

"The cleaning crew said they saw no one in the building— and they go into every room except the supply and checkout rooms. There's no place to hide in her office—if a killer *was* in the building, they would have seen him. He *could* have hidden in the supply or checkout room, but—" and he turned to her, "he couldn't have come out after the crew left and made it to her office without setting off the motion detectors or being seen by the cameras. That equipment is real sensitive—picks up the slightest movement. And the office windows are sealed."

He sighed and turned over, raising himself on his elbows.

"They already looked over the surveillance videos. It shows the cleaning crew arriving and leaving; every person who went in came back out before they activated the alarm. A little later, the system picked up someone in a hooded coat who used a key to open the door and deactivated the alarm using the supervisor code. The interior system got a clear shot of her face from the moment she came in until she went into her office."

"What about what happened in her office after she went in?" asked Megan quietly, not wanting to recall the scene. "There's a camera in there, isn't there?"

Zack frowned.

"Lilly said Parnall told her that one wasn't working. The company says it was called in for maintenance two days ago and they hadn't gotten around to sending anyone to fix it."

He shrugged his shoulders.

Megan wasn't quite ready to let it drop.

"But, Zack, you *know* she didn't kill herself! *I* know she didn't kill herself! *She wasn't holding a straight-razor!* All three of us saw the same thing, didn't we? How can they see anything different?"

Zack closed his eyes as though he were too tired to continue.

"I don't know, Megan," he replied and he yawned.

"I think it isn't so much what they saw as how they chose to see—" he suddenly cut himself off as he realized what he was saying. Bolting upright with a wild stare, he slowly raised his hand to his neck and felt it wonderingly.

"Baby?" asked Megan quickly, alarmed at the look on his face, "is something wrong?"

He looked at her strangely.

"Is there something wrong with my neck?" he asked, raising himself up so she could see it in the light.

She raised herself up as well and carefully looked it over with her eyes and fingers. Then she kissed it and responded, "No. It looks fine. Why?"

The same expression was still on his face.

"Mark—"

Her alarm increased at that name.

"What about him?" she asked sharply.

"He asked me if I had bad dreams last night," said Zack, slowly.

Her worry instantly passed to annoyance.

"What's that got to do with your neck?"

He looked straight at her.

"He looked at my neck this morning. Acted all strange like he saw something wrong with it. And then asked me if I had bad dreams last night—" and his voice faded.

Megan stared at him mutely, her lips slightly parted, not daring to breathe.

Zack suddenly pushed the blankets aside and quickly got out of the bed. Megan lunged forward and grabbed at him. He stopped, turning to look at her.

"Where are you going?" she cried out.

"I—I'll be right back. I have to check something—" he muttered and, shaking her off, dashed from the room.

Megan, tense and alert, heard him walk across the living room followed by the unmistakable sound of a computer starting up. She sighed irritably and turned over, muttering under her breath.

She became less worried and more annoyed the longer he remained at the keyboard. At last, her patience gone, she flung the blankets off and swung her feet to the floor. A noise in the doorway made her look up angrily and she started with fright.

"Baby?" she asked, quavering.

Zack stood motionless in the doorway for nearly two minutes, his haggard face flooded with terror. Then he slumped forward in a faint just as she leaped to her feet and caught him in her arms. Supporting him with all her strength, she steered him back toward the bed, muttering, "Baby! It's okay!" over and over, trying not to let her voice betray her feelings.

She managed to get him under the covers at last and joined him, pressing herself close to him, shuddering as she touched him: his body was as cold as a block of ice.

When he did not respond she grew frantic and forced herself to warm his body with her own, anxiety flooding her thoughts. At last, he reached out his hand and clasped hers tightly in his fingers. She collapsed on top of his chest and lay there, holding him closely, trembling.

"Zack!" she cried out softly, "Zack, Baby! What's wrong? What—" and she fell silent at the look on his face.

He stared at her.

"Megan?" he said, finally.

"Yes?" she answered.

"You know that book Mark is always reading?"

For some reason this question struck fear through her heart. "Yes," she nodded.

"Do you know what the title of that book is?"

She just stared at him, nearly holding her breath.

"What is it?" she asked finally.

"Isorropia," he said, softly. She stared at him uncomprehendingly.

"What does that mean?"

"It's Greek for *'**Balance.**'*"

Megan turned white to the lips as she suddenly recalled Mark's license plate, raising her hand to her open mouth with an expression of dismay. Zack, exhausted beyond endurance, pulled her to him and closed his eyes. Then darkness swept over him, mercifully blotting out the scene.

ABOUT THE AUTHOR

Brian Monroe (1959—) has been writing fiction since the age of nine. He penned his first serious endeavors during his sojourn at Western Washington University, culminating in the novel, *Cypress Park* (1984). Following a fallow period during which he served in the United States Air Force, he began writing in earnest during the first years of the twenty-first century, including short stories such as, *The Sabre-Toothed Rabbit* (2009) and *Trapped in Boirac's Coil* (2010). He favors the horror/mystery genre spiced with occasional gleams of dark humor. He currently resides in a forgotten corner of the Pacific Northwest.

For more information, including preview and pre-publication announcements, please visit the web page at:

http://books.bass-x.net.